Dear Readers,

This book has had a strange and wonderful life.
Strange, because when I began writing about my
mentally handicapped brother Alfred, I expected it to
be hard, digging around in those early memories, trying to tell as true a made-up story about him as I
could. Instead, it was as if the story were waiting in
the wings to be written. I never knew from one
chapter to the next what I would say, yet it flowed out
of my heart and through my fingers in one long easy
thread.

Alfred was an old family sorrow. We all thought
of his life as damaged, a waste. Yet, because of this
book, all that is turned around. Its many readers
have told me over and over that it has changed their
way of thinking about the impaired. His life was not
a waste after all. He has reached out and touched
more people than most of us do. Such is the power
of words, and if that isn't wonderful, I don't know
what is.

Jan Slepian

The ALFRED SUMMER

Jan Slepian

Philomel Books • New York

Copyright © 1980 by Jan Slepian
All rights reserved. This book, or parts thereof, may not be reproduced in any
form without permission in writing from the publisher,
PHILOMEL BOOKS,
a division of Penguin Putnam Books for Young Readers,
345 Hudson Street, New York, NY 10014.
Philomel Books, Reg. U.S. Pat. & Tm. Off.
Printed in the United States of America. Published simultaneously in Canada.
First published in 1980 by Macmillan Publishing Co., Inc.
First Philomel Edition, 2001.
Library of Congress Cataloging-in-Publication Data
Slepian, Jan. The Alfred summer / written by Jan Slepian. p. cm.
Summary: Four preteen outcasts, two of them handicapped, learn lessons in
courage and perseverance when they join forces to build a boat.
[1. Friendship—Fiction. 2. Handicapped—Fiction. 3. Courage—Fiction.]
I. Title. PZ7.S6318 Al 2001 [Fic]—dc21 00-053741
ISBN 0-399-23747-X
1 3 5 7 9 10 8 6 4 2

ACC LIBRARY SERVICES
AUSTIN, TX

To my parents, and
for David

The ALFRED SUMMER

Chapter One

My mother holds open the door and says, "Let's go, Lester. A nice walk in the schoolyard," Sometimes she says, "You can play there." I wait for it. Do I say, "What? Go to the schoolyard with *you*? I'm fourteen years old! Are you out of your mind?" Do I say, "Sorry, Ma, not today. I got football practice this afternoon . . . a flying lesson . . . a dance engagement?" Not I. I'm glad to go. Can you imagine having two directly opposite feelings at once? I'm glad to go and at the same time I hate it. The only things I can juggle are feelings, and I'm an expert.

So down the elevator, across the street and into the schoolyard we go. I stay close to the fence and pick my way through the popsicle sticks and broken pieces of cement. What a mess, like picking my way through a mine field. Like the princess and the pea in the fairy story, she couldn't sleep because of the pea under Christ knows how many mattresses? Well, I could be sent spinning by an innocent little pebble. Me and the princess. So I stick close to the wire fence, my own little bouncy mattress.

1

Meanwhile, She follows. Actually, it may look to all those old chair-sitters across the street as if we are separated, two distinct bundles happening to be going the same way. "What is she, lost?" they wonder back and forth, those old ones taking the sun and commenting on the world. "What does she want in a schoolyard with the kiddies?" they say. I'm an expert in knowing what people say. They may not even know they are saying it, but they are just the same. "And look, look at that other one, that poor little *tsotskela*, poor fella. He shouldn't be allowed. What's he got? St. Vitamin's dance? What's the matter with him?"

Of course, they see us almost every afternoon. They know it is Mrs. Klopper taking her crippled son out for a walk. Maybe they say "spastic son." The fancy ones will say "cerebral palsy." Though it does look like I'm taking her for a walk instead of the other way around. Me in front and She behind. What they don't see are the strings attached. Some are attached to my bobbing head, some to my waving arms, thousands to my drunken legs. Like spider webs they are—felt, not seen, impossible to pull free even if I wanted to.

"Hey!" I shout in my head to the chair-sitters. "What you see here is the Great White Hunter taking her pet puma out for a walk. He needs his blood meat for the day and you're IT!" I spring, they scatter, and a volley ball bounces against the fence nearby. The shock of it jangles me and the puma falls, knocked over by the breath of a ball.

Myron Kagan picks me up, his fat red face lumpy with pimples and distress. "Gee, sorry, Lester." He really is.

Also he smells like a dirty clothes hamper. "Are you okay?" He wants to get back to the game.

Now here's the thing: I want to say, sure I'm okay, or, that's all right, I'm fine. Something like that. Well, if he has an hour or two to spare I'll get it out. I might in that time be able to tell him what's on my mind. In other words . . . in other words I have no words. Or none that I can get out without looking as if I'm strangling. At least with people I don't know. I have millions . . . billions! inside me, but if I try to say hello and you're a stranger, you have to wait awhile. A little patience, please. I can say it, you understand, but I have to choose which wires to pull to make things work and that takes time. Besides, the effort sets up the jangles. Then the old arms wave and I get all tippy toes, stepping from one foot to the other. I look like a puppet whose manager has just been goosed by lightning. Funnneeee.

Ma glares at Myron as if he had just clubbed me and stolen the diamonds. "Why don't you watch out what you're doing, you maniac!" She's ready to kill. Her flabby face that I know so well disappears, the soft, reproachful "Who me?" or maybe it's "Why me?" expression I also know so well is gone. The bewildered eyes now blaze, and *Aha!* . . . the Avenger stands there ready to do battle . . . for me.

Poor Myron. He can't look at her. "Sorry, Mrs. Klopper," he says to her shoes. He picks up the ball, itching to get back to the game. Voices are calling him. "C'mon, c'mon." "Let's go!"

Ma sees the game for the first time, and I know the worst is coming. Her voice turns wheedling, her eyes greedy. "Maybe you would like Lester to keep score? You can use a scorekeeper. Go on, Lester. Go play. Go keep score." Aw Ma. Aw Ma. My neck cranes and I get out the "No!" faster than usual. They want me to keep score like they want a rat bite. All she wants is to see her boy play normal. All I want is . . . nothing.

We go on. She picks up the threads. Giddyap horsie!

The schoolyard is busy this afternoon. The girls are out there jumping rope. "Down the Mississippi where the steamboats push." I love to watch this, the rhythm of the rope and the chant quiet my nervous nerves. I chant, too, and inside my head it all goes smoothly. Roller skaters are out in full force today. A screaming stick ball game is going on somewhere in the middle of the playground. Bike riders and runners weave in and out. Jacks players are on the sidelines along with the watchers like Ma and me. Then the heaving moving mass in the middle. Colors ride with the movement, and all at once I feel such a rush . . . ! The sun streams across the living playground and even the tan, ugly apartment houses lining the street across the way seem homey and good to me today. Heads poke out of the windows, Mamas all of them, resting on their forearms, leaning out and visiting. Their voices are lost in the general hubbub, but as I said, I know what people are saying. So I know that they are saying . . . nothing much. Hello, how are you, I'm sick, I'm not sick, stuff like that. It all seems so fine to me suddenly. As if it were all arranged somehow that on a certain summer afternoon in the year of 1937, this playground, my street, maybe the whole of Brooklyn, maybe even the whole world was, or could be, just right for seconds at a time. I know it is just the look of things, and, well listen, once again I'm an expert—an expert at not trusting the look of things, not judging that way, not people, not anything. I'm an expert because . . . look at *me*. My outside doesn't tell you a thing about what's really going on. Anyway, I enjoy these few moments of feeling that everything is just right, and what seems to be . . . *is*. It doesn't happen often.

I breathe deeply, smile my smile that only She knows is one, and we go on, circling the playground.

I nearly trip again, blocked by a kid squatting over a Dixie Cup cover. He turns it over and over, examining it as if it were a treasure map. I watch him. He doesn't seem to notice me or anything else around him. He drops the round cover and then reaches out for an old Lucky Strike cigarette wrapper. This time he knows just what he wants. He starts peeling off the tin foil. But in order to do this he has brought a much smaller fist to help hold the wrapper down. And that small fist doesn't seem to work right. Well, well. What do you know? Not that I would call a bad hand a weighty problem.

I say, "Hi."

He looks up at me. Dark eyes look at me without interest. "Yeah, hello," he says, and returns to his peeling. He's only a year or so younger than I. What's he playing with an empty pack of cigarettes for?

I ask him. A long sentence for me with a stranger.

He looks up at me again, and again his eyes register nothing. Or at least nothing that I'm used to. Like embarrassment (how do I talk to this dummy?) or impatience (how do I get out of talking to this dummy?). He just looks at me, smiles and says, "Oh, I'm just pickin' off the foil."

He holds a piece of the torn foil up to me and says, "Look here, look here, I wanna tell you something." Chuckling, tickled at what he is about to show me, he pulls a small ball of foil out of a pocket. It's about the size of a golf ball, which means he's picked over a lot of cigarette wrappers in his day. "See? You see this? I make a big ball of foil and then Mr. Apatow at the candy store gives me two cents for it. What do you think of that, hey?"

All this is said to me in such a confidential, proud way you would think he was telling me the best secret in the world.

Was he kidding me? No, he wasn't kidding. And there was something else. I could tell he didn't even notice that I am . . . what I am. Either he didn't notice or he didn't care, which is odd enough. What is odder is that in this skinny kid, black curls, dark eyes and blubber lips, the inside matches the outside. That is, nothing else was going on inside him while he said this. I can tell, I can tell. He was all of a piece.

Suddenly it appealed to me to help collect the tin foil for his ball.

I wait for the "No, thanks."

He says, "Yeah, yeah," not giving a damn one way or the other. That makes me feel . . . easy. I can speak.

"What's your name?" I ask.

"Alfred," he says. Doesn't ask mine, but I tell him anyhow.

My name is repeated from behind me. "Lester, come

6

away from that boy," says She. Loudly she says this, as if he's deaf.

I stare at her. She, who is forever pushing me onto one boy after another, one squirming disinterested victim after another, now says get away.

She comes up to me and again, without bothering to lower her voice, says, "He's retarded, can't you see that? He's the retarded kid from the house at the corner. Leave him alone. He's not for you."

She has picked up the strings. This time she is ahead and I follow. So that's it. Retarded, is he? A true dummy. I look back at him sitting against the fence, completely absorbed in peeling his foil. No wonder She pulled me away. *Her* son has to play with Normal. It would make *me* normal. That's a hot riot. Well, what do I care?

We step along, the rush of pleasure in the day left back there with the Dixie Cup cover.

I hear irregular footsteps behind me. Then beside me is Alfred, smaller and lighter than I first thought . . . and limping. God, he has a limp too? Bad hand, bad foot and also a dumbbell. What a prize.

"Say, Lester . . . find any?" he asks, the ball of foil in his hand. I waggle my head.

"Say, Lester, you wanna see my stamp collection? C'mon, I'll show you." His limp isn't bad, really. Just a bit draggy. If he stood still, stuck his bad hand in his pocket and also shut up, no one would know. Stamp collection? He probably doesn't know a stamp from a cowflop. Still . . . .

She turns around, sees us and says, "Go away, Alfred. Go home now. Go." Like shooing away a fly.

7

He looks at her with big eyes. No anger, no fear, just looks at her.

He nods his head. "Yeah, sure." Ready to do as he is told, no grudge.

He smiles at me, waves and limps away.

"So long," I call after him.

The threads pull me away. Giddyap horsie.

Chapter Two

Alfred awoke. He looked over at his parents' bed to see if his mother was awake. They were both still asleep. So was Richy, his little brother, still asleep on his cot across the room. Alfred turned on his side to look out the window. From that third floor window he could see the whole schoolyard across the street. No one was there yet. He mulled this over. If nobody was in the schoolyard, and Mom and Daddy and Richy were still asleep, then it must be early. If only he had a watch he would know what time it was. He could tell time easy. Maybe he could get out of bed and see what time it was from the big clock in the hall. No, Mom said don't get out of bed until I say so. He could go to the hall and look at the fish tank. See the pretty fish. He could feed them. Oh yes.

He pushed the light blanket down with his foot and slid off the bed, careful not to stumble on the bed so close to his own. The one small bedroom was jammed with beds, leaving only a narrow aisle to the door. Once in the hallway it was much darker and he needed to pat one side of the wall with his hand to guide him. He knew it was six pats to the kitchen, no pats while passing it, then six more to the end where the hallway opened up to the living room. The curved wall clock was above the fish tank. But he had forgotten his interest in the time. The tank was lit, bubbling away. The tropical fish, with their swirling tails and bright colors, held his complete attention. He took the box of fish food and sprinkled some on top. It didn't seem anywhere near enough. He sprinkled the whole box, covering the surface with the flakes. The fish began to feed and he watched, fascinated.

"The boy is up, Flo."

"Mmmmmmmmph?"

"The boy is up." He patted her shoulder, kissed it and turned around.

"Oh God, what time is it? On a Sunday, too, when you can sleep." She climbed over Alfred's father, drew on a robe and padded out to the hall.

"What are you doing up?" she whispered. "You know you are not to get up till I tell you to!"

Without taking his eyes from her, Alfred pointed to the fish tank. Clumps of fish food clouded the water like a paperweight snowstorm.

"You gave them the whole box! Wait till your father sees this!" her voice rising, strained. She glanced into the living room. Another bed, another body. "Your Aunt Ida's still asleep, you bad boy, you. So are the rest of us. Now get yourself back to bed and stay there."

The look from his eyes stopped her. "Oh, get along," she said softly, smoothing his curly hair and giving him a little push. "I'll fix it with Daddy. Today we all go to the beach. Daddy will take you into the water."

Everything else was forgotten and he smiled with

open-mouthed pleasure. "Yeah, yeah, and I can sell my magazines."

She smiled because he did. "We'll see."

She looked after the limping boy. Then stood for a moment looking at nothing, waiting for the familiar weight, labelled Alfred, to settle down inside her. She thought of it as a rather puffy little bag the color of a mushroom, swinging from a lung perhaps, or maybe a rib. Somewhere where the breathing is. She was never without it.

"Hi, Mom, I'm hungry."

"Richy!" He had startled her. "What's the matter with everyone this morning? Why are you up?" She couldn't keep the irritation from her voice.

Richy paid no attention to the edge in her voice. "Alfie bumped me and I got up. What's for breakfast?" His round face shone with good nature.

"Well, come on in the kitchen. I'll get the sandwiches started for the beach. Uncle Murray and Aunt Horty are coming, and maybe Aunt Fanny and Uncle Ben."

"Ooooh . . . Leila, too?" Leila was Fanny and Ben's daughter, just his age, but she bossed him around as if she owned him. Richy adored her.

"What do you think? They'd leave her home? Of course, Leila, too. Now go brush your teeth and I'll make you some scrambled eggs."

Richy was the bench saver.

At Brighton Beach on a sunny Sunday, the Gold Rush was on. The gold was a bench for the day. There were dozens of them strewn across the broad beach, but never enough for all. The most prized, especially if company were coming, were the few double benches arranged back to back. The race began early in the day. An empty bench would be sighted and an entire family would then run for it, all hands and armpits loaded. They sprinted across the hot sand to stake their claim before another family, also running, also loaded, beat them to it. Then the big umbrella was raised and under this striped roof the family moved in. They spread out on the bench as if they had a year's lease. Beach chairs were set up for the nappers. Card tables unfolded for the players, blankets spread, toys unpacked and food poured out of paper bags.

Richy was good at bench saving. He got there early enough to get a double and then straddled the benches, defending them against all comers until the rest of the family arrived.

"This is taken, lady. My family is coming right away."

"What? Both sides already? Some nerve. We'll sit."

"No, no, lady. Ooooh, I see them. There they are!" He waved wildly to a distant family he didn't know at all and managed once again to save the bench until the next challenger made him go through the whole thing again.

As soon as his family arrived, he raced off to the water with Leila. Alfred, his magazine bag already slung across his chest, watched his father put up the beach umbrella. His mother and aunts were unpacking, settling in for the day.

"Can I go, Mom?"

His Aunt Ida knelt to tighten the laces on his high black sneakers. "Do you think you ought to let him go, Florrie? It's a hot day, you know."

His mother called over to his father. "Do you think Alfred can sell his magazines today? Do you think it's too hot for him?"

"Let him go, Flo. Let him go. He's not a baby. He'll come back to the bench if it's too hot. Right, son?"

"Sure, Dad." He would know exactly where the bench was, never getting lost, ever, any place he had ever been. It was a talent he had, so confusing to his parents. He was so good at remembering telephone numbers and birthdays. He even knew all the stops of the train from Brighton Beach to Gimbels in New York, where his mother took him for his special shoes. So how could he be so stuck at a younger age than he was, so backward in some ways? It was as if a clock had stopped inside him.

Already grinning, Alfie nodded at, but hardly listened to, the string of instructions. Yes, he would check back at the bench in an hour. Yes, he knew where the clock was, no, he wouldn't go into the water alone. Finally he could turn and be off.

He trudged across the sand, heading for the covered arcade that ran the width of the beach perpendicular to the water. He mingled with the strolling crowds doing what he liked best to do: make money. "*Collier's*, mister? *Saturday Evening Post*? Five cents." He was a familiar figure on the beach, so there were many people to say hello to, though no luck with the magazines.

The walkway was paved and wide enough for several lanes of body traffic. It was much easier for him to walk there than on the sand. Besides, it was roofed over, so it was cooler than on the open beach. He headed in the direction of the water. Someone brushed by in a hurry and Alfred stumbled. A hand reached out to steady him. "Oh, hiya Myron."

"How ya doing, Al?" said Myron, licking his ice cream cone and never for a moment taking his eyes away from the girls passing by.

"Come on, My, let's go," said one of the twins, Myron's younger sisters who were fat blonde replicas of their brother. Even the bulging blue eyes were identical.

"Hiya, Shirl," Myron called out to a girl fresh from the ocean. She was still wet, flicking the drops from her arms to her laughing, ducking friends. She never turned her head.

He stepped out and flicked a heavy finger on her shoulder.

"Last touch!" he said and offered his favorite one-sided smile plus eyebrow lift practiced in his bathroom mirror.

"Ow!" The girl stopped and rubbed the red spot. "What's the big idea? You crazy or something, Myron Kagan? That hurt!"

"Uh, hiya, Shirl," he said again, the smile fixed on his face like a frozen tic.

"See you around, Shirl," he said to her back.

He looked after her until Alfie touched his arm. "Your sisters went that way," he said.

"Oh. Oh sure. So long, Alfie." Myron moved on.

Alfred limped along towards the ocean. The walkway ended where the sand began its long gentle slope down to the water. Alfred stopped there, looking at the ocean before him, the sun glinting off the water, making him squint. He could see heads bobbing in the water, but the slope of the sand hid the shoreline. Sometimes, after a wave broke on the shore and the foam sank into the sand, the sea left gifts. Once he found a matchcover for his collection. Sometimes there was a bottle he could return for money.

He walked along the hard packed sand at the water's edge. He walked with his head down to see what he could find. His canvas bag, still full of unsold magazines, bumped his side. His sneakers were getting wet, but he didn't seem to notice. Too many people were in his way. He had to weave around them. Now and again he stopped to pick up a shell or a stone or a bottle cap, but there was nothing to keep. He trudged on.

Lester watched him pass by. He sat on the sand at a comfortable distance from other people and waited for his mother to finish taking her dip.

"Hi, Alfred," called Lester.

"Yeah, hi," said Alfred, not taking his eyes from the sand.

"He doesn't know me from one of those shells," mumbled Lester to himself. He wondered what Alfie was looking for and kept his eyes on him.

Big boulders lined the shore at the far end, marking the boundary of the pay beach. Beyond it was the free beach. The rocks spilled along the shore, one piled on the other like some giant's set of blocks. Full of hidden crevices and sudden waves crashing against them, the rocks were dangerous. A sign posted nearby said so.

Chapter Three

Alfred saw the fluttering of a cigarette wrapper caught in the fold of a rock. The shine of the foil drew him and, even though it meant a climb, he headed for what he wanted. Nothing was on his mind but that. The first rock was easy, like stepping up some stairs. He forgot the magazine bag weighing him down, forgot warnings, possible danger or his waiting parents. Up another boulder and across, then up another one. He was almost within reach and he had eyes for nothing else. Because of that, his foot went into a hole and he crashed to his side. Luckily, the canvas bag broke his fall, but the side of his face was scraped and bloodied the great stone. He struggled to free his foot. When he could not, he gave himself up to the rock as if it were his bed. He didn't make a sound. Pain never bothered him at all. It was as if he didn't know what it was. It never occurred to him to call for help.

Lester saw it all. He was the only one. He struggled to his feet, pierced with alarm. He tried to call out to the man standing along the shore watching the horizon, but could not. Urgency was blocking him. He stumbled to the man and pulled at him trying to point to the rocks. His arm would not obey him. He tried to pull him closer to the rocks. Maybe he would see Alfred. But the man pulled himself away. "Sorry, kid, I don't know what you want, but I haven't got it. Let go." He headed for the water. Lester got himself to the walkway. People looked at him curiously and then stopped. They could see something was terribly wrong. The alarm Lester felt was sounding without speech. He could see Alfred caught in the rocks forever and he, unable to help . . . . A small crowd gathered, asking questions, making it worse. Lester was desperate and the more desperate he felt, the less he was able to control any part of him that could tell what was wrong. When he saw his father push through the crowd, he burst into tears.

"It's all right, folks. I'll take care of it. He's all right, perfectly okay," said his father, sweat on his bald head, too embarrassed to meet any eye. Nobody budged; the show wasn't over.

In a low voice he said to Lester, "What the hell is it now? Calm down. Take a deep breath and for God's sake calm down. Where's your mother?" He looked around for her, frantic to escape the scene. So seldom was she apart from her son that he jumped to a conclusion: "It's her? Something happen to her?"

Lester said no and, fighting for control, was able to tell his father about Alfred. "You mean there's some kid caught in the rocks? Where? Show me!"

At that moment Lester heard a voice coming down the walkway calling, "Alfred? Alfred?" Mrs. Burt was searching for her son. Lester clutched his father and repeated the name. Mr. Klopper understood and immediately went searching for the voice.

Now Lester heard his own name called from the other direction. His mother was also searching for her son. "Lester? Where are you, Lester?" She tore through the crowd thinking the worst. Her relief at finding him intact made her yell at him and embrace him at the same time.

Lester's father returned with Mrs. Burt. Quickly, they all moved to the rocks, followed by the crowd, which was not about to leave until the drama was over.

Mrs. Burt tried to climb to her fallen son but could not. She could only see a leg, a canvas bag, *his* sneaker. Panic at his stillness made her legs tremble. Myron and Mr. Klopper made their way over the rocks to Alfred while she watched, each breath a small moan. He was still lying where he fell, like an offering to the sky.

"You okay, kid?" asked Mr. Klopper, freeing the foot. "Sure," said Alfred, totally unsurprised at seeing them. Myron, strong and solid, picked him up, bag and all, and soon put him down beside his mother.

"Hi, Mom," said Alfred, smiling as if awakened from a sleep. "I couldn't get down." His scrapes had clotted and his trapped leg was stiff, but whole.

He submitted patiently to an examination of his body for bruises, to the minor scolding that went with it and to the hug of relief that followed it. Mrs. Burt poured out her thanks to Lester's father and to Myron and especially to Lester. She pressed Lester's mother's hand and told her, "Your Lester saved my boy. Just saved him. Maybe the tide would have come in, or a big wave . . . ." She pulled Alfred closer and, terribly aware of the group of listening strangers, tried to smile at him as if she were entirely herself and this were a party they were politely leaving.

"Thank these nice people, Alfred. Thank them for finding you."

"Thank you," he said dutifully, more interested in checking the magazines in his bag.

Mrs. Burt said, "Wouldn't it be nice if Lester came over to visit sometime? You could show him your collection." Her face was alight at this new idea: a friend, a friend for him. Never had he ever . . . . She turned a face of hope and eagerness to Lester's mother. "We would love to have him," was all she said. The "please" was unspoken but hung in the air.

"Now come the excuses," thought Lester. But Mr. Klopper interrupted. "I'm gonna get back to the handball game, Mae," he told his wife. To Mrs. Burt he said, "Nice to meet you. Glad everything turned out okay." He hurried away.

The crowd was dispersing now that the show was over, turning away with a faint air of disappointment.

Lester watched the stocky figure of his father stride down the walkway. "You could have said *something* to me," he thought bitterly. "For once you might have said a good word. I did a good thing just now, and you . . . . Shit!" He turned back to the conversation. Resentment and an unnameable longing churned in him, beat against his ears so that he could hardly hear. He saw that his mother had taken some money out of her beach bag and was handing it to Myron. What was she up to now?

". . . and treat yourself to some ice cream," he heard her say. "And why don't you take Lester with you?" she added.

As if he had heard a joke, Alfred laughed. "Hey, Myron, you just had some ice cream, right? I just saw you. That's a good one!" He seemed tickled at the idea that anyone could have two, one right after the other.

Myron smiled sheepishly back at him. "That's right, Alfie, you remember all right. Come along and I'll share with you."

Mrs. Burt shot Myron a glance that made Lester's hot heart melt.

"That's very nice of you, Myron. I know he'd like that. I don't have my pocketbook with me, otherwise . . . ." Myron awkwardly indicated that wasn't necessary. To Alfred she said, "Let me take your magazines back to the beach. No more selling for you today, young man. Are you sure you feel perfectly all right?"

Alfred was sure, eyes only for Myron. "I want you to come back to the bench right after the ice cream, you hear?"

Mrs. Burt didn't repeat the invitation for Lester's visit. She said a polite good-by to Mrs. Klopper and once again thanked Lester profusely.

"I'm in love!" thought Lester. "She's the nicest lady I ever met." He looked at Alfred with envy. "She stayed nice even though she had him." He suddenly felt exhausted from all the emotion of the afternoon.

His mother said to him, "Lester, don't stand there like a stick. Are you half-asleep?" Asleep! Is that what he looked like? His mother continued hectoring. "Go on now. You and Myron are going to the cafeteria for ice cream. I'll come get you in a while, so don't go away. Wait for me. Go on now."

She shooed the three boys away. As the trio moved up the walkway, she watched, her lips compressed, her head nodding. *Her* boy walking with others filled her gaze.

Lester, walking along, was uncomfortable and rather puzzled. "You don't have to do this," he said to Myron. "You can go now. I'll take Alfred." He was so intent on freeing Myron from what must be an awful trap for him that he was able to talk more freely.

Myron had never heard him say anything before. It surprised him. It sounded to him as if Lester had a mouthful of mashed potatoes, but he understood even so. Besides, it was as if his mind was being read. He *was* wondering what he was doing with these two, acutely aware of how funny he must look with them limping along at either side.

"Naw, that's okay." It seemed to be the most familiar situation in the world for him to be doing something he didn't want to do. "Myron, do this, Myron, do that," from his mother, his sisters, even his grandma. And so he was always looking away from where he happened to be, only part of him there. That was why if there was a glass of milk to be spilled, he spilled it. If there was a door to be walked into, he did. "My son, the *shlemiel*," was his mother's summation. He gave the most pleasure to his younger sisters because they knew how to tease him into a frenzy and then escape his rage with delighted screams. Myron was inarticulate, shy, clumsy; his sheer bulk got him into games but not to parties.

21

Naturally, he didn't notice when he stepped on a piece of wool hanging from the knitted beach coat of the woman walking in front of him. Not only did he step on it, his toe caught in the knot. It was slow going on the walkway, having to match his step with Alfred's limp on one side and Lester's weaving on the other. Myron was busy dreaming a favorite daydream of his. It was more than a dream; it was a plan. He thought of it as an escape hatch, a way of getting away from "Myron, do this" and "Myron, do that." It occupied all his thoughts. The traffic of bodies up and down the walkway pushed past the three of them like cars on a freeway. The woman ahead was talking animatedly to her companion. She moved on, but her dangling piece of beach coat did not. It stayed on Myron's toe, and so her coat began to unravel. Little by little, rows of the white wool disappeared, swallowed up like kernels of corn from a cob. Myron stepped along, utterly oblivious, thinking his thoughts, his foot stepping on the wool, pulling it as it touched the sandy cement.

Lester saw all this happening, fascinated. Laughter burst from him in little jets. He tried to get Myron's attention but could not. He couldn't walk and talk and laugh at the same time.

The lady finally felt the tug of the wool. Still chatting with her boy friend, she reached around and felt the damage. A piece of her beach coat was missing!

Lester thought Myron handled the whole thing with the greatest aplomb. He looked down at the mashed wool under his foot with utter bewilderment, ignoring the abuse heaped on him by the outraged lady. Slowly, he untangled his toe and handed her the dirty bundle as if returning something borrowed for a moment. Lester thought for one wild moment he might even say "Thank you" for the loan. Evidently, the return of the wool seemed to Myron to be all that was called for. No apologies, no "I'm sorry," nothing but giving back what wasn't his. "C'mon," he said to the two boys and they continued on to the cafeteria, leaving the lady still holding the filthy clump, her turn to be bewildered.

Chapter Four

Once it had housed a merry-go-round, but all that was left was the circular building. The heavy roof and small windows darkened it, so that when you came in from the sun it was as if you had entered a tunnel. It was a popular place at the beach, a place where you could buy your lunch and sit on a regular chair and eat at a real table. The cafeteria was full of clatter and echoes. The noise seemed to drift up to the ceiling and spray back down, covering all below with a mantle of sound.

The three boys paused in the doorway to get used to the dimness and to the noise.

"You guys get a table and I'll bring the ice cream," said Myron.

"I want soda," said Alfred.

Myron looked at the change in his hand. "I don't have enough." He considered for a moment. "Okay, we'll share a soda."

Lester and Alfred wove their way around the tables looking for one that wasn't taken. Lester felt that people stopped in mid-sentence, even in mid-chew as they passed. He felt they left a trail of silence in their wake like smoke. Here we come, folks, the Cripple Parade, he thought, a real conversation stopper. He saw that Alfred was utterly oblivious of the stares. If the price of comfort is dumbness, then I'll take dumb, he said to himself. Yet he felt a twinge of protectiveness towards Alfred, as if he wanted to throw a blanket over him to hide him from the gapers. Not himself so much as Alfred. He had never felt like shielding anyone before. His mother flashed in his mind.

"There's one," said Alfred, pointing to an empty table near the wall.

Myron soon joined them and they sat in silence, Lester concentrating on getting the spoonful of ice cream to his mouth, Myron and Alfred passing a bottle of cherry soda back and forth.

"You go to school?" Myron asked Lester. It was just something to say. He never imagined other people's lives. He had never been this close to anyone who couldn't even eat ice cream without effort.

Lester was bracing his arm on the table to hold it steady so he could bring his mouth down to the spoon. He swallowed and said, "No, someone comes and teaches me at home."

"Luckyyyy! No school." He shook his blond head with the wonder of it. "You can do what you want."

"Noooo, I get taught. I like to read a lot."

"You do?" Again he shook his head. He shifted uncomfortably in his seat as it occurred to him that Lester wasn't a regular person, and so that was why . . . . But then, he was just talking to him as if he were.

He looked at the palsied boy who for that moment was in repose. Myron realized he wasn't all that bad looking when he stopped jerking around. He was reminded of someone foreign, one of those English boys from a fancy school like he'd seen in the movies. Lester was fine-boned and tall. The straight fair hair and sharp nose made Myron think of the word "aristocratic." He turned to Alfred.

"Do you?"

Alfred was concentrating on sucking the last of the soda through the straw.

"Do what?" he asked.

"Do you go to school?"

"Yeah, sure. I gotta A in conduct. My father doesn't like it when I bring home a bad report card." His face clouded. "Sometimes I do."

"Where's your school?"

"Across the street, you know, across the street is the school. They have ungraded classes and I have Mrs. Milwit. I mean, this is summer so I don't have her now." He was very earnest in explaining this.

Myron remembered seeing lines of odd-looking children of all ages waiting to go into a classroom when he went to that school. They all had something wrong with them, he remembered, but he didn't pay much attention.

Lester had finished his ice cream. "Do you play football?" he asked Myron. He was beginning to feel just fine. He saw himself sitting at the table having this conversation, a real conversation just like the rest of the people in the cafeteria. "Do you play football?" he said again, just for the pleasure of asking.

26

Myron was not looking at him anymore. He was watching two young girls coming towards him. His sisters.

"Ooooooh, we caught you! We've been looking all over. Where'd you get the money?" asked Loretta. She plopped down in the wire chair next to him and lifted the bottle of soda to see if any were left. Her twin Lorraine grabbed it out of her hand. "I'll just take this for the deposit," she said, tucking it into the top of her bathing suit. "Ma wants you," she told Myron. "She wants you to come to the bench right away. You have to walk Grandma home."

Myron's red face got redder. "Why don't you? You could walk her same as me. Why always me?"

"Well Ma wants *you* and har, har, har," said Loretta.

"Last touch!" cried Lorraine, smacking Myron's head with her open palm. They ran away before he even thought to grab.

Myron sat brooding for a while, the other two silent and sorry. Myron clenched his fist and thumped his thigh as if the frustration that filled him came from that spot.

"Boy, someday . . . . " he started to say and then trailed off.

"Yes?" Lester wanted him to go on. He saw that Myron was choked with feeling. He sensed turmoil and couldn't understand why. Surely not just because of some teasing sisters. To him Myron had everything, everything! So how come he was sitting across from him bursting and unhappy?

Myron didn't answer all at once. His whole manner changed. He sat thinking about something that pleased him, the rage entirely gone. He seemed to have decided something and leaned over the table, now eager and excited. "Listen, you guys. I'm gonna tell you something I haven't told anyone yet. It's a secret, see? I'll tell you and you don't tell anyone else. Got it?"

The other two nodded solemnly, their eyes wide, fixed on him.

"Well, I'll tell you this. I'm building a boat." He leaned back in his chair, waiting for them to be thunderstruck.

They were.

Alfred was tickled. He wagged his head and chuckled, "A boat, gee, a boat." He had never heard such a wonderful thing. If it were sitting there before him it couldn't be more dazzling. To him it was an accomplished fact. "Gee whizz, a boat."

Myron glowed at Alfred's admiration. He couldn't have chosen a better person to impress.

Lester was so filled with questions he didn't know what to ask first. What do you mean a boat? What kind? Where are you building it? What for?

Myron was ready to answer questions all day. "In the basement of our building I got it. There's a room there where the super stores paint and he's letting me use it. I'm building this boat all by myself. It's a rowboat, and believe me, it's going to be a beauty. A real beauty I'm telling you." He smiled at them, he smiled at the ceiling, the walls and everyone in the cafeteria, silly with pride.

But Lester still didn't understand. He realized that Myron was entirely serious and was building a rowboat in the basement of his apartment house. But then what? He was somehow going to get it to the beach and launch it in the ocean? And then what? Row to where?

Myron was impatient with talk about *where*. "It

28

doesn't matter where. I'll just be able to row myself out in the ocean." He clasped his hands on the table and stared down at them, as if they would help explain what he felt. "I'll be out there where it's quiet, see? Quiet. Nothing can . . . nobody can get to me. Have you ever been out in a boat?"

Lester and Alfred shook their heads. He might as well have asked them if they'd ever climbed a mountain.

"Well, when you're out there, you look back to shore, then everything is so tiny. All the people and houses look like little ants. They are nothing." He snapped his fingers. 'Just nothing but far away and don't matter a bit. See? I mean, in the boat I can get away. You know what I mean?"

He really wanted to know if they understood him. Lester nodded his head, yes. Alfred, watching Lester to see what to do, also nodded yes.

Yes, indeed Lester knew what Myron meant. In plenty of daydreams and night dreams, too, he had gotten away. Only in his case it was his body he escaped from, something that being out in a boat wouldn't help. He still didn't understand what a boy like Myron needed to get away from.

Myron slammed his hand on the table. "I'm going to do it. Do you think when I'm out there they can get to me? I would laugh. Ma could say, where's Myron the klutz, and I'd be gone. Myron, do this, Myron, why can't you do that? And my sisters? . . . Gone. Left behind. Ants, that's all. And not only them . . . everything. Everything." He made a sweeping motion with his hand, as if it was all too much to explain.

The table was silent, the tirade over. Then the idea of

the boat filled Myron once again and he said, "I got some wood, see? And I'll get a lot more. It's all around the neighborhood just for picking up. Every night after supper I go down there and work." He was excited again.

The excitement was contagious. Lester felt it like a wave lifting him up, carrying him along. He was gripped by longing. Most of all he wanted to prolong this new sense of being a part of someone else's concerns. He felt like a child asking this, but he didn't know how else to say it. "Let me help." He indicated Alfred. "We could both help."

Myron said, "Naw." How could they help? They couldn't even lift a hammer. Thinking about it he said no again.

The flat no sat on the table like a fence between them, a fence the two boys were completely used to.

The silence pressed Myron to add. "Look, this will take a lotta wood, see? I find some in the empty lot, you know, the one next to my building. I hafta go all over the place—in the alleys and all. And carry it back. It's heavy. See what I mean? There's no way that you . . . ."

His baffled, troubled face moved Lester to say, "That's okay, Myron."

It was Alfred who said, "I see lots of wood when I sell my magazines."

"You do?"

"Yeah, lots of wood. I know where I can find it, but I can't carry it on accounta my bad hand." He held it up for them to see the logic, not for sympathy. He wasn't trying to change Myron's mind, just offering facts.

Lester said, "I have my wagon I always use to carry things in. If Alfie shows me the wood we can bring it to you. You'll save time."

Myron saw it. "Yeah, I'll save time." He nodded at them and slapped the table with an open palm. "Okay then. That's it. If you want, find me wood and bring it down the basement after supper. I'm there most every night. If you wanna help, it's okay."

They grinned at one another, the three boys dazed by what was suddenly between them. Lester could hardly look at either of them. It was almost a relief to hear the old familiar call from his mother. "Lester? Lester, where are you?"

He stood up so she could see him. He had a secret. It burned him.

"Why are you so flushed?" his mother wanted to know when she came close. She put a hand to his forehead. "You have a fever?"

Satisfied that he wasn't ill she said, "You boys enjoying yourselves, huh? Talking baseball maybe? Go ahead, talk. Don't mind me."

She pulled a chair over from the next table and sat down. Myron suddenly remembered his Grandma. He struck his forehead and got to his feet in a hurry.

"Wow, I gotta go! Am I going to get it! So long, Les, so long, Alfie."

Till that moment he hadn't noticed that Alfred had already slipped away.

Mrs. Klopper looked around the empty table and sighed. "Come Lester, we go too. Your father is impatient already."

31

Chapter Five

After the gloom of the cafeteria, the strong sun made Alfred dizzy. He leaned against the green slats of the building, idly watching the people going in and out until he felt better. The sight of Lester's mother at their table reminded him of his own. He wanted to get back to the bench to see her. She was the pull of his everyday thoughts, the natural focus of his daily life.

He limped along the walkway until it was time to cut across the sand. Along the walkway, racing towards him, were several small boys. They were darting in and out of the crowd, whooping it up, ready for fun in whatever shape they could find it.

They found it in Alfred.

Several of them were Richy's friends, so Alfred was someone they knew.

"Hiya, Alfie." They pushed against him and one another, their little bodies wet and sandy.

"Race you to the water, Alfie." This drew a big laugh. Alfie joined in.

"Ooooh, your sneaks are untied!" Alfie looked down but they seemed perfectly okay to him.

"No they're not," he said as if the answer would be comforting to the mistaken child.

"Hah, hah, April Fool!" cried the child. "April Fool!" yelled the others.

Alfred knew a good joke when he heard one. "April Fool is in April, right? And this is summer already. That's a good one on you!" He laughed and shook his head at how ignorant some people can be. He stepped around them and onto the sand.

"So long," he said.

Silently, without a word of planning, the youngsters followed him. They formed a line behind him, each one limping like him, each one, like him, holding one arm bent at the elbow, hand dangling. Alfred had no idea he was being followed. He had no idea he was the leader in this game of Follow the Leader. This was fun for the little boys for a while, especially when they discovered that it was even funnier if they exaggerated the limp and made faces at the same time. But soon the game began to pall and they stopped. The April Fool boy motioned the others to come closer. He had something to tell them. When they heard what it was, they burst out laughing. Once again they followed Alfred, this time chanting loudly, "Al-fred, Al-fred, toi-let pa-per! Al-fred, Al-fred, toi-let pa-per!"

This Alfred heard. He had no idea what the children were up to. But he sensed *toilet paper* was a bad word said like that and his mother wouldn't like him to say bad words. He laughed uncertainly in case it was a joke and said, "Naw, naw." He waved them away and moved on. He knew the bench was nearby and he looked for a familiar face. The boys were still chanting "Al-fred, Alfred, toi-let pa-per!" when he came upon his family.

His father, hearing it, sprang from the beach chair. The moment the small troup saw his face, the chant died. Alfred's father grabbed the first thing that came to hand, a newspaper, and ran a few steps towards the fleeing boys, swinging it as if it were a weapon. If it were a cannon he would have used it.

"Git!" he shouted after them. "Get out of here, you little bums!" His face was white and his eyes blazed with anger.

He turned them on Alfred. "Why didn't you tell them to stop. You're bigger than they are. Don't let anyone push you around, you hear me?"

From the other end of the bench Mrs. Burt heard him scold Alfred, saw that familiar, bitter look on his face. She knew, as usual, Alfie must have done something aggravating and immediately spread imaginary skirts for him to hide behind. She hurried over and said, "Whatever it was, remember he had a bad fall on the rocks this morning. Maybe he doesn't feel well." She took Alfred's hand and sat him down on the bench.

"Your head hurts, doesn't it?" she said encouragingly. Sickness excused everything.

"Naw, I'm fine, Mom. Can I have a sandwich?"

This was his Aunt Ida's pleasure. She delved into one of the many paper bags and pulled out a bulky sandwich bundled in waxed paper. "Here you are my darling, one corned beef coming up."

Richy was playing "Flash Gordon" with Leila at the foot of the bench. As usual, she was Flash and Richy was his girl friend Dale. He had heard what the children had called Alfred. He had seen his father's response. Abruptly, he left Leila and sat closer to his parents, who had moved away from the bench so the others wouldn't hear.

His mother stood facing her husband, hands on her hips, ready to fight for her son.

"What is it this time? What got you so angry?"

Alfred's father shrugged and said, as if he were tired to death, "Nothing, Flo. Leave me alone. If you didn't hear what went on, that's fine with me. But I'll tell you for the thousandth time, you'll never get anywhere protecting him like this. He has to learn to stand up for himself."

This made her wild. "Stand up for himself? He can hardly stand *by* himself! Cruel! That's what you are, cruel to your own son! You push him and push him and push him and you know he can't do it!"

"Sure I push him. You think that's cruel? Wait till you see what the world will do to him. Then you'll see what cruel is. I push him so he can do better. *Be* better. Make him try harder. Not baby him all the time like you. That's not helping him!"

"He *needs* protection!" Mrs. Burt cried. "I want to make life easier for him, not harder. It's hard enough!" She was too choked to go on.

Richy, sitting on the sand nearby, was frightened by their fights over Alfred. And this time he had something terrible on his conscience. It was his fault they were fighting.

His father noticed him, saw his stricken face and grabbed him up in his arms. "Let's go, son. We are going in the water right this minute. You can dive off my shoulders fourteen-and-a-half times."

Alfred's mother watched them go off and burst out to her sisters, "Look how different he is with Richy!"

One of the sisters tried to soothe her. "He has his reasons, Florrie. Whatever he does it's for Alfie's sake, you know that. He loves the kid—and you, too. C'mon, cheer up. In a hundred years you'll laugh at this. Help me pack up. We have a long trip back to the Bronx."

At this, Alfred took his attention from his sandwich and said plaintively, "I want to stay and hear the band, Mom. Can't I? They're going to play soon. Can't I stay?"

It was true. The bandstand was beginning to fill up with the orchestra. The little round building, like a cupcake on stilts, was the Sunday afternoon treat. It sat in the middle of the beach, the sand beneath it already crowded with people waiting for the music.

Aunt Ida said, "I'll stay with Alfred, Flo. Let the kid watch. He loves it so. We won't stay long."

Mrs. Burt merely nodded and began packing for the walk home. She wanted to go home alone and sit on her chair and close her eyes.

Aunt Ida and Alfred found a place to sit close enough to the bandstand so that they could see and hear. Alfred began smoothing the sand between his legs, going over it again and again. Then he smoothed the sand beside him, slowly, absently, always in circles. He would stop his moving hand only to applaud, or to nudge his aunt as he did just then. "Look, there's my friend Myron. He musta come back."

"A friend? Where, dear? Show me." This was something new. Never had Alfred spoken of a friend before.

"Over there."

36

Just then the orchestra began to play. The music was lively and soon there was a group of boys and girls dancing under the violent sun, hopping like sand fleas.

Myron was on his feet, watching the dancers, moving around like a restless bear. He circled the flailing arms and legs and passed close enough for Alfred to throw some sand on his legs. "Hiya, Myron."

Myron looked down, then wedged himself next to Alfred, not noticing that he sat on a piece of blanket.

"Excuse *me*," said the girl next to him, pulling at it, trying to get it away from underneath his thick body. Myron didn't notice the struggle. She had to push his shoulder to get his attention. "Hey, you deaf? You're sitting on my blanket!" The two other girls with her giggled. Myron lifted himself up a bit so she could pull it out. He smiled with quickening interest at them all. "Uh . . . sorry. Uh . . . you listening to the music?"

"No, we're watching the football game." More giggles from the girls at this stroke of wit. Alfred was interested. "What football game?" he wanted to know. "Hush," said Aunt Ida.

"I bet you're a good dancer," said the first girl, dying to dance, no matter with whom, just so it was a boy.

Myron made a face. "Naw. Me dance? Not on your life. It's stupid!"

One of his sisters came up to him then and whispered something in his ear. He shook his head no. She spoke to him again and pointed somewhere behind her. He got to his feet, turned away from the music and the dancing and the girls to follow his sister across the sand.

At home that evening, Alfred's aunt asked her sister, "Did you know Alfie has a friend upstairs?"

"Who's that?" Mrs. Burt asked as she headed for the kitchen, her hands full of dishes.

"Some boy named Myron. Is that his name, Alfie?"

He was leafing through his stamp collection on the floor in front of the radio. "Yeah, Myron. That's his name."

"Of course I know Myron. He was the nice boy who helped Alfie this morning. They had ice cream together."

Alfie suddenly remembered something he had meant to tell his mother. "Hey, Mom, you know what?" He sat up smiling. He had a great piece of news for her. "I'm going to help Myron build a boat. Inna basement. Tomorrow night he said for me to come down after supper. Okay Mom? Can I?" He had altogether forgotten it was supposed to be a secret. He didn't know how to keep anything from her.

"Don't be silly, child," smiled his mother. "You don't mean a real boat. But anyhow, whatever it is, you can go down for a while."

She turned to Richy, who was leaning against his father's chair, looking at the newspaper over his shoulder. "Why don't you go next door and play with Sheldon for a while? You can get out from underfoot while we get the dishes done."

Richy didn't want to go, which was unusual for him. What had happened with Alfred was still on his conscience, making his stomach ache. "I don't want to, Mom, I want to listen to the radio. Amos and Andy are coming on."

"But you usually listen with him. Go ahead."

"Aw, Mom, I don't want to watch his mother pick his nose again."

Mrs. Burt turned, not believing what she had just heard. "What did you say?"

Now he had the attention of everyone in the room. His father put down the paper and his aunt came in from the kitchen, her hands still soapy.

"That's what she does, all right. She lays him on the bed and picks his nose with her finger." He looked around at their unbelieving faces. "I saw it! Lotsa times I saw her do it. Honest. Eccchhhh!" He leaned over, pretending to vomit.

All at once the room was filled with laughter. The three grownups looked at one another, the appalled laughter shared.

Richy was pleased with his offering, but the bad feeling inside wouldn't go away. He longed to confess to his father, but he couldn't bear to have him angry with him. What he wanted to tell him was that it was his fault that the boys yelled "Alfred, Alfred, toilet paper" that afternoon. He had told his friend Jerry from the first floor how Alfred used so much paper he stuffed the toilet many times. And now that rat Jerry was one of the boys that afternoon and must have told. If his mother knew, she'd have a fit. Always something over Alfred. Why couldn't he have a regular brother?

Chapter Six

I hated it when She fussed over me in the cafeteria this afternoon. Right in front of the others. Feeling my forehead as if I were a dribbling two-year-old instead of a dribbling fourteen-year-old! Usually I don't care. It doesn't mean a thing to me how she fusses. She says, "Come," the strings are picked up and I come. She was right about one thing though. My father was impatient. Very. By the time we changed in the locker room and met him at the beach gate, his cigar was chewed like a piece of meat. Also, the eyebrows were wagging. Those are my weather signals, those brows, my private barometer. At rest, it's fair weather, leave the umbrella home, folks. If either up or down, watch out! I'm afraid of those brows. I'm afraid of him. So is *she*, but when it comes to me, she goes her own way. Why not? He has abdicated after all. The King has abdicated and left the running of the government—me—to the hoi polloi—*she*. But only when it doesn't interfere with his pleasure.

"It's about time!" he grunted when we showed up at the gate. "C'mon, let's get out of here, Mae."

Usually he goes on ahead, not wanting, not able to

stand my slowness. Usually we walk the few blocks. But today he took the car because we were going on a special outing and he wanted to get home in a hurry to change and to rest. He had a business meeting tonight with other insurance men at Lundy's, the fanciest restaurant in Sheepshead Bay, the next town over from Brighton Beach. They guzzle oysters and talk about their debits over clam chowder. Over the lobsters and beer they talk about premiums, eat cheese cake and swap dirty jokes over coffee. This is all my own imaginings, of course. I have never been to one of my father's business meetings. For that matter, I haven't even met a business acquaintance of his, since we have never, ever, had company home that I can remember. He would have to introduce me. "My son, my heir, the perpetual motion machine." No, no, we won't be joining the gentlemen.

That evening Ma and I were dropped off at Coney Island, a short drive from the restaurant. It's our biggest treat.

As soon as we got out of the car our ritual began. We always start off with a frankfurter from Nathan's, laden with sauerkraut and mustard. Delicious! Then we cross the street to the big merry-go-round, walk that whole side and return on the other.

The calliope on the merry-go-round was going full blast, but there weren't any kids on it yet. I was glad for that. It's a ride I can go on if I sit on one of the gilded chariots instead of a horse. Afterwards, after that pleasant dizziness goes away, I sometimes find a brass ring or two dropped by some butterfingers onto the wooden floor. It means a free ride. I didn't find any tonight, but I did see something I wanted far more. I saw a piece of wood. Wood for the boat! I could begin helping right away! But where would I put it? In my ear? Ma would never stand for me carrying it around. She didn't want me even to talk to Alfie. Whatever would she do if she found we were in the lumber business together? No, I had to pass that old board by as if I didn't hear it cry my name.

What I hate are the freaks. Tonight the barker was out front on the small stage, his hat pushed back and his cane marking time with his spiel.

"Come on in, folks, come on in. You are just in time to see the most amazing sights of your life. They have to be seen to be believed, yessirrreeee. Just in time, folks. The show is just starting. Inside we have . . . " smack goes his cane on the painted canvas picture above him, "the Alligator Boy!" I see four claws and a tail, the body of an alligator and the head of a cheerful young boy. Smiling, yet. God!

The barker continues, knowing that the crowd eats all this up, fascinated with misery. "Inside, inside, the Fat Lady!" Smack goes the cane. "Six hundred pounds of love and joy, ladies and gentlemen. And her boy friend, the Thin Man." Smack. "If he turns sideways he disappears."

Now the barker's voice gets confidential. He invites the crowd to step closer, he has something to say he doesn't want the children to hear. The children immediately make a dash for the front. "For ladies and gentlemen only, a medical wonder! A sight you'll never forget. Jean-John, half man, half woman. Yes sir, born in one body." The crowd pushes closer, not wanting to miss a word. "This unbelievable sight, and you will see it all, nothing hidden, this not-to-be-believed sight is . . . inside!"

Smack goes the cane. There really is a picture of a half man, half woman up there. One side has long hair and tits, the other side looks like a regular man. I wonder if it can do it to itself.

"While you are lined up getting your tickets, ladies and gentlemen . . . and children of course, I will give you a taste of the wonders inside. Pip and Flip, those lovable twins with the little pin heads. Pip and Flip, come out here."

Out come these pathetic creatures, long dresses, skimpy hair pulled up to the tops of their tiny heads and tied with a ribbon, old, old, they filled me with horror. They shuffled about on the small platform, grinning in some mindless way, while the barker played the harmonica. I was frantic. I pulled at my mother's dress and we walked on, leaving the freaks behind. All too close to the bone.

It's Luna Park we want to get to. That's the climax of the night. The arch of colored lights spelled out the name over the entrance. In a niche on one corner of the entrance sits a big wooden doll, a mechanical lady. She wears a checked overflowing dress, her head tied in a bandanna and she rocks back and forth, her red-painted mouth wide open. She is in a perpetual fit of laughter. I can never not join her when I hear it. My mother and I looked at one another and laughed too. There is a truce between us on these nights.

43

We found our usual bench and, while licking our custard ice cream cones, watched everybody who went in. It was dark by then and I was glad to be out of the way. Sailors were out in full force tonight, some ship in port. Their arms were always around girls carrying kewpie dolls or stuffed animals won at something or other. Lots of kids pushing and shoving and horsing around. I found myself thinking, that's all right, I've got a boat to think of. I've got Myron and Alfred to think of.

At the entrance there's a big barrel turning around and around. You have to go through that moving barrel in order to get inside. I'd never make it. I'd be there forever. They'd have to send in food, set up a bed, toss in some clean clothes and my birthday presents.

From our bench we could see that, once past the barrel, people have to walk across a swaying bridge, one side to the other. Just beneath the bridge is a clown sending up jets of air from a hose. The women scream and grab their skirts, but not before we all get a good look. I expect the clown pays Luna Park for the job. One time I saw some hair. Tonight not so lucky.

We sat and watched until Ma looked at her watch and said that we had better start back.

We crossed to the other side and watched the Cyclone riders for a while. They say that's the fastest, highest, most scary roller coaster in the world, and I believe it. The screams sound as if they are all being tortured, but there are lines of people waiting to get in, so I guess it must be fun. I'll never know and I don't miss it.

Who needs a ride on a roller coaster when just being in Coney Island on a summer night is one big ride? My eyes and ears and nose have the time of their lives, working hard, trying to take it all in. What a jumble of smells and noise! I know just a few streets away, on the other side of all this, lies the dark boardwalk and ocean. If I turned the corner it would be like leaving a wild party for a church. It's hard to imagine the quiet. I smell the ocean, the fine seaweed smell. But it's all mixed up with salt water taffy, hot dogs, bodies, french fries and God knows what else. Each ride pumps its own music or has its own barker out front, shouting his own invitations. But that's only background for the uproar people can make when they are out for a good time.

It's all jumping with life! And I'm always amazed to find it so each year. Sometimes we come here in the winter and it is so positively dead you can't imagine it ever being like this. Like seeing a bare tree in February and returning to it in full leaf in June. A miracle.

As we walked along, heading back to the car, I saw coming towards me a string of girls, holding hands, taking up the whole width of the sidewalk. They were making people duck under their arms to get past. I tried to bend in time, but I couldn't make it. Flat on my back I landed, fast and easy. I looked up at a ring of faces. "Just part of the show, folks," I wanted to say. "I'm paid to do this." My mother was dividing her time between me, all worried concern, and the girls, all fury and scorn. She too could be up on the poster with the half man, half woman. Smack goes the cane. "See the half-love, half-hate lady!"

One of the girls helped me up, but that didn't stop Ma from shouting, "Roughnecks! You shouldn't be allowed!"

The girl who helped me up said, "Sorry, Charlie," and

smiled at me, waiting until I was steady before she ran back to her friends. She seemed . . . nice. In fact, the whole incident was okay. I wasn't hurt and I was attended to by a girl. A big moment for me.

I was a mess, sidewalk filthy, oozing ice cream and other junk on my pants and shirt. That's what my father said when we got to the car. One look at me and he smacked the car wheel. "He's got crap all over him, Mae! He's covered with it. Christ!" She got some napkins from Nathan's and while cleaning me off explained in her soothing-the-beast-tone what had happened. She has some plateful to take care of, my mother, when you think of it. She has to fight the whole world for me, or so she thinks, while at the same time woo whoever she thinks would be useful to me. Then she has to keep the old man's temper down because, get this, because somehow it's Her Fault that I'm this way. And along with this she has to keep the strings between us in good shape at all times. Actually, I do my share of keeping those strings attached, I know. But the difference is that I know they are there and she doesn't. How I wish I either didn't need them or that, like her, I didn't know they are there.

When the napkins cleaned me up enough, I climbed in the car. As we drove along she asked, "So how did it go, Manny? How was the dinner?"

That's the right approach. We hear in detail how the lobster was not as good as last time but better than that time he got so sick from it—remember, Mae? Yes, sure she remembers. How could she forget? Wasn't she up with him till all hours? And who was there?

Well, this brought out all the heartiness in my father.

One thing I really admire about him is that he likes his work and genuinely enjoys the company of people. He's a great card player and jovial teller of jokes and visitor of sick friends. To hear about it, he has many. My mother and I just don't happen to be among them.

"Danzig brought his boy along tonight," he told us. "What a kid." Admiring shake of the head. "Can you imagine—head of the hockey team, a straight A student yet, and he also has the time to copy his father's collections in the black book? What a boy. A real *mensch!*"

I'm home in bed and yet that word keeps going around in my head. *Mensch.* A real *mensch.* A real man. No, not a man, a real person, a real human being. Only for my father this means: Be a *mensch*—come in first. Be a *mensch*—don't cry. Be a *mensch*—hold your head up. All he admires in the world is wrapped up in that word. Lester, you're a real *mensch.* Thanks. Don't *mensch*-un it.

I fall asleep with that girl helping me up. "Sorry, Charlie," she said.

Chapter Seven

"So where were you again this afternoon?" Lester's mother wanted to know. They were in the kitchen doing the dishes together after supper. They were alone for, as usual, Mr. Klopper had pushed back his chair after dessert, looked at his watch and said, "I have to go, Mae." Lester never remembered hearing an explanation of where he was going, or his mother asking for one.

"We haven't been to the schoolyard for a long time," she said, handing him some silverware to put away. "All of a sudden you're a busy man, my son. You getting tired of your old mother?" This was said playfully, lightly, as though passing it off as a joke would hide the anxiousness.

Lester didn't answer. "So where were you?" she repeated. Other days he had just said, "Out for a walk." This time he was ready to tell her. "With Alfred."

"Alfred?" She was really surprised. "You mean that retarded from the corner house? The one with the bad hand and foot yet? You saved from the rocks?"

He nodded and then held up his uncontrolled arms for her to see.

She understood him. "So what, Lester! So you've got a condition, too." Her soapy hands pushed back the hair from her worn face, stern and intent with the need to make him understand, "But you have a mind, Lester. A good mind." She nearly crooned the word. "I know how smart you are. So they should know, too. You understand what I mean? Do you know what I am saying? Lester, Lester my son, listen to me. You will never get anywhere hiding away, staying with the backward. What do you get from such a boy? Nothing!"

Lester looked at her and shrugged. "I like him," was all he said. How could he explain why Alfred was important to him? Wandering around the neighborhood with him in the afternoons, looking for wood, finding pieces here and there to put in the wagon for the boat, he was content. He was at peace in the company of the limping boy. Everyone he knew, his parents, Myron, his teachers, people on the streets, in the newspapers, Christ! the whole world was struggling. Struggling to have more, to *be* more, fearful and striving. Except Alfred. As for his own good mind? What a laugh. "No one sees my mind, Ma," he said, wanting to take her from the subject of Alfie. "They see only this." Once again he held up his arms.

His mother wiped her hands on the dishcloth, the dishes done. She leaned her back against the sink, untying the apron from her big body. "You don't give them a chance," she said, quietly now, with a conviction that shook him.

He was about to say, "Listen, if even my own father can't get beyond this . . . ." But his mother looked at the kitchen clock above the door and abruptly started hurrying.

"I'll be late for my mah-jongg if I don't get a move on. It's at Mrs. Weitz's downstairs in 3D tonight, in case you want me. What are you going to do with yourself?"

"Oh, I'm going over to Myron's," Lester said casually. He knew this was like telling her he had a date with the pope. He was right. Immediately his mother's face brightened.

"That's nice. Real nice. Myron's a good boy, a fine boy."

Lester could see Myron was about to grow wings. She gave him a kiss and as she hurried out the door said, "That's more like it, a friend like that!"

Oh, sure, thought Lester, a friend like that is so good for me. He is so great he is building a boat in his basement so he can sit in the middle of the ocean just to get away from his lovely normal life. Hey! A thought struck him. They had been talking about what to name the boat. Now he had it.

He knocked on Alfred's door. Mrs. Burt opened, smiled and invited him in. "Lester's here, Alfie," she called.

Alfred was sitting in the living room at the card table looking at his stamps. Lester had discovered that he really knew the stamps, recognized which ones to put together and sent away for ones he wanted. He knew Alfred was a born collector of things, of stamps, match boxes, tin foil, bottle caps, marbles, anything tangible that could be put together in the same category. Wood was just another thing to collect. He was the one who pulled the red wagon and whose sharp eyes found the best pieces.

Alfred looked up. "Hiya, Lester," he said, and looked

down at his stamps again, his attention fixed on them. Lester could never get over how Alfred took his presence for granted, never surprised to see him, as if he lived in the fish tank in the hall and had just emerged to keep the family company.

"Lester's here to go down with you to see Myron in the basement," said Alfie's mother gently. Mr. Burt looked up from his paper, "Go on, son," he urged. "I'll put your stamp book away. Good evening, Lester. How are you tonight?" Mr. Burt's courteous attention made him nervous. He stepped from foot to foot and managed, after a struggle with his breath, to say, "Fine."

Mrs. Burt came out from the kitchen with a package, which she tucked into Lester's pants pocket. "Cookies for later," she said. Her face glowed with pleasure. Lester's heart flopped over as usual in her presence. He understood how glad she was for Alfred to have a friend. "To her, I'm the special one," he thought. "*I'm* the one with wings in this house."

The two boys left together and took the elevator down to the basement. That afternoon they had stored their wagon, filled with wood, down in the room where Myron was building his boat.

He was there now, in the large paint room, bending over what looked like a coffin in the making. It sat on two sawhorses in the middle of the dingy room. A single, naked light bulb hung down from the ceiling, casting its harsh light on Myron at work. The rest of the room was dim. Old paint cans and brushes of all sizes sat on the shelves that lined the room.

"I was wondering if you were coming tonight," he said

51

as they walked in. He wiped his sweating face with a dirty forearm and, with hammer in hand, pointed to their wagon piled with wood in the far corner.

"Is that what you brang for the boat?" he asked. Not waiting for an answer, he pulled the wagon close to the boat so the light would fall on it. He went on, "Now I want to explain something to you guys. The wood you brought the other day was fine. This here is no good. Well, some of it is, some of it ain't. This piece is no good, this no good, this one okay." He was sorting, tossing short ones in a pile in the corner and the longer ones stayed near the boat. "What I need now is longer pieces, see? I'm workin' on the sides and I need as long as you can get, see?"

He was the seasoned skipper explaining to his green crew what a good master boatbuilder needed.

Lester told him that he knew long pieces were best, but they were hard to find. And he thought the smaller pieces might be handy when it came to making the front and back.

Myron examined the boat as if for the first time he realized it needed two ends. "Oh, sure. You're right. We need smaller pieces, too." He was very agreeable that way, not minding suggestions, or even criticism. He was used to criticism.

The two boys sat on overturned paint drums and watched Myron work. It was quiet in the basement, not even street sounds coming through the small high windows. Only the inner workings of the building could be heard, like stomach noises—the rumble of plumbing or the clanking of the elevator. Myron hammered and occasionally cursed as he missed a nail but not his thumb.

Once in a while he would point to a piece of wood. "Hand me that, will you?" Alfred would eagerly get up, hand it to Myron and go back to his paint can.

Myron reached for one of the long nails he kept in a jar at his feet. He straightened up and said, "What's that?"

Footsteps. Nobody came to the basement that time of night, nobody. Something white flashed past the door. "I saw something," Alfie whispered. They heard a voice say, "Come back here, Mr. Moskowitz! Where are you?"

All three were frozen in place, staring at the doorway. A girl appeared in it carrying a small cat in her arms.

"Wow! You scared us," said Myron.

"Sorry, Charlie," said the girl, looking around the room curiously. She leaned against the doorframe, stroking her cat. "My cat ran away and I had to find him. Say hello to everyone, Mr. Moskowitz." She held up one of the small paws and waved it.

Alfred thought that was hilarious. "What a name for a cat. Mr. Moskowitz." He wagged his head and looked at Lester to share the joke. He always looked first to Lester.

"Well sure," smiled the girl. "He's the one who gave him to me, Mr. Moskowitz did, this afternoon. He owns the grocery on the avenue? He let me bring him home. Of course I couldn't really bring him home," she added. "My folks won't let me keep pets in the apartment. My dad says a cuckoo clock is the only pet he'll allow in the house. Don't you think that's funny?" She giggled and looked around to see if the joke was appreciated. "So I'll keep him down here. Mom lets me take him milk and I'll visit him every chance I get."

Lester was staring at her. He knew her! "Sorry, Charlie" was what she said when she helped pick him up at Coney Island that night. He wanted to tell her. To remind her. But he wasn't ready to talk yet, too tied up with the coincidence. He didn't have to remind her. She noticed him, looked him over and said, "Say, aren't you the one we knocked down in Coney Island, me and my friends?"

Lester could only nod yes.

"Yeah, I was out with my track team that night acting crazy. I'm sorry about that." She grinned at him and winked.

Then she left the doorway and circled the boat. "Say, what's going on here?" she asked Myron who was back at work, hammering. "Sombody die? Somebody died and you're going to bury him in this, right?"

Myron couldn't have been more injured if she had run him over with a truck. "This is a boat we're building here, you dope. A boat. And no one is allowed in here except us. I'll call the janitor!"

"Wait a minute. Calm down. I didn't mean anything. Honest, I didn't know. Hey listen, the super doesn't know Mr. Moskowitz is here and he won't let me keep him either. I know. I've tried plenty of times before. That's an okay boat. I mean now that I know it's a boat, that's an okay boat." She whistled in admiration at such an okay boat.

Myron was still angry. You could say anything about him, but not his boat. He looked her up and down coolly and said sarcastically, "Say, are you supposed to be a boy or a girl?"

It was true, there was nothing girlish about her, her thin childish body in a pair of white torn running shorts and a man's undershirt several sizes too large. Her straight brown hair came to her earlobes and looked as if she had cut it herself without looking. All her features were sharp, firm, no softness anywhere. Her movements were quick and nervous. Like a little fox, thought Lester. Only her eyes, as she turned them on Myron, were soft, but clear and utterly direct.

"Yeah," she said agreeably. "Everybody has trouble sorting that out." She bent over her cat, cradled in her arms. "But I'm a girl just the same, aren't I Mr. Moskowitz? And I'm going to be the fastest girl runner in the world someday. Just like Babe Didrikson. All my friends say I look like her, only skinnier."

I can believe it, thought Lester. Look at those legs. Like pistons.

Alfred knew what running was all about. "I saw a good runner once. We have track and field at school and our whole class was allowed to watch."

The girl nodded as if that were an important piece of information missing in her life until that very moment.

She *is* nice, thought Lester. I knew it right away.

She said to Alfred, "I've seen you around. What's your name?" Lester could tell she knew about Alfred. He told her. "Alfred. Alfred Burt."

"And what's yours?" she asked Myron.

"And yours?" Lester's turn. For the life of him he couldn't get it out. Myron spoke for him. "That's Lester," he said, watching the girl carefully. She was still on trial. Not taking her eyes from Lester she said, "Say, are you shy, or what? Don't you talk?"

Myron spoke again. "He doesn't talk so good with strangers. He's spastic is what it's called."

The girl whistled once again, and said, "Hey, that's

tough." Very matter of fact she was. "Well, I'm Claire, in case anyone is interested."

Then she turned her full attention to the boat. She wanted to know all about it and asked questions until Myron was completely thawed out. It was his favorite topic. The only thing she didn't understand was what he was going to do with it once it was built.

"You mean to say you want it just so you can get away from all the things that bother you? I mean from your folks and all? Not just to have it, just like that?" She was genuinely trying to understand.

"Well, don't you ever feel . . . mad?" Myron asked. "Look at you, the way you look and all. . . ." He meant she flunked the girl test.

"Well, sure. But, well, I mean, I have a pretty good time anyway." She was at a loss to say why she wasn't miserable, but all she knew was that she wasn't.

"It's not just my family," Myron said. "I don't want you to think it's just that. It's well, girls, you know—other kids—uh, *everything*." His voice was thick, he felt thick all over with the hopelessness of explaining how he felt, of being understood.

"Oh, sure, everything," she echoed doubtfully. Then she said, "Well, now you have the boat. That's in the 'everything' isn't it? Things can't be all bad if you have this." She patted it.

Myron didn't think this was worth an answer, but started working again as if nothing else existed.

She found a paint can and sat on it stroking her cat, rubbing her cheek against the fur. Lester pulled out the cookies Mrs. Burt put in his pants pocket and passed them around. Myron stopped working and sat with them. They all munched for a while, the room peaceful again. Then Lester, feeling at ease, was able to bring up a subject he had on his mind since early evening. "What are we going to call the boat, Myron?"

It was their favorite question. Always one name or another would appeal for a moment and then be discarded as unworthy.

Myron said, "At lunch today I thought maybe *The Golden Dragon*. What do you think, fellas?" He repeated the name a few times and then he himself said, "Naw. That's no good."

Alfred said, "My father showed me a picture of a boat called the *Robert E. Lee*. It was inna magazine. That's a good name for a boat."

No one bother to comment.

Claire said, "Of course, I haven't had time to think much about this, but it just came to me. You know Lindbergh? *The Spirit of St. Louis*? His plane? Well, how about *The Spirit of Brighton Beach*?"

Lester had been waiting for his chance. Before Claire's name had a chance to sink in he said, "I have one. Tonight at supper . . . . Listen. We can call it *The Getaway*. *The Getaway*. That's what it's for, isn't it?"

Myron pounced on it. "Hey, that's good, Lester. I like it. *The Getaway*." They all chanted the name a few times, louder each time. Myron was elated. "It sounds sort of tough and it's just what I want!"

The paint room was suddenly full of talk, the excitement of the moment binding them together, making the room seem brighter, themselves comrades in arms. They all turned to look at the boat, their common cause, not seeing the nails sticking out, the jagged ill-fitting wood, the grim shape. An unlikely thing to have triggered such a strong current of feeling.

Myron put his tools away for the night. Claire wanted to know if she could come again, if she could help build. After all, she was going to be coming down to see Mr. Moskowitz every night anyway.

"Sure, kid," said Myron as he snapped off the light. They all trooped over to the elevator.

Lester was struck by how easy Myron was with Claire, not at all what he expected from Myron's moans about himself and girls. "That's because he doesn't see her as a girl at all," thought Lester. "He can be himself. Even so, he's blind is what he is."

Chapter Eight

Thereafter the four of them met in the paint room almost every night. The routine was much the same and that was what they liked, the routine of it. Lester and Alfred sat on their paint cans, watching the work, fetching when needed, sorting when asked. At some point in the evening Claire appeared with Mr. Moskowitz in her arms and, if she stayed, the talk would quicken, for she brought with her a restless energy. Slowly the boat grew more boatlike, although a corpse would still find it homey. Myron did the actual work, and as he became more familiar with nailing and fitting pieces of wood together, he became more adept. Sometimes he could go through a whole evening's work without smashing a finger. Claire's uncle owned a paint store and she was certain she could get paint when the boat was ready for it. Myron knew where he could get some oars. It was all shaping up.

They never knew what to expect from Claire. Sometimes she would show up just to feed Mr. Moskowitz and then leave with a wave. "So long, got a meeting of my club. See ya." Sometimes she would practice her running starts across the paint room. There was a night when she came down in a gorilla mask and didn't take it off the whole night. "What mask?" she kept saying. "I'm not wearing a mask. What do you mean mask?" Many nights she just sat quietly with her cat on her lap telling stories. She made up wild tales about the strange countries they would visit rowing the boat from one shore to another. Out of this grew their favorite game of shipwreck. Whole evenings were spent deciding what they would eat, how they would live when they were marooned on a deserted island.

Claire was full of stories, loved to tell them, loved to hear them. She was able to get Myron to talk as no one else ever had.

"Since Pa died, I gotta do everything around the house. No kidding. She keeps saying I'm the 'man of the house' now. So what does that mean? I get leaned on and leaned on and if I don't do things right, scream? You'd think I stabbed her instead of forgetting to take out the garbage." Myron hunched his shoulders in the telling as if guilt was sitting there, a heavy backpack. No wonder, thought Lester, he wanted to shake it all off. No wonder he wanted to get away, to sit out in the ocean and have it all become a speck in the distance. It was all too much of a burden. Lester remembered thinking once that Myron had everything.

But the stories weren't all grim and little by little Myron could see that.

"So this morning my kid sister Lorraine runs into the apartment, starving, and having to go. You know, pee."

He looked quickly over at Claire, suddenly remembering she was a girl. He would rather drown in it than say to an ordinary girl that he had to go to the bathroom. "She has to go through the kitchen in order to get to the bathroom. So she stops to get something to take with her. When she opens the icebox . . . you don't know my mother, how she piles things in, stuff falls out, you know? . . . She catches a bowl of something in one hand, something else in the other. And as she is standing there, both arms full, she has a real hurry-call. She can't wait. She dumps everything on the floor and runs to the bathroom. Now get this"—Myron got angrier and angrier as he told this—"I'm in the bathroom, see? Don't I have a perfect right? She bangs on the door, I have to get out that very second or else she's going to die. So I get out. I really do. She runs in and the next minute I hear a scream. I run back in and there she is, her feet in the air, stuck in the toilet bowl. I, I was the one who left the seat up. Of course the seat's up when I go! What does she think? She didn't notice . . . and so when she sat down she fell in. And who's to blame? Me, that's who. It was my fault! Can you beat that? You should have heard the yelling!"

He looked around for sympathy. What he got was a burst of laughter from Claire. "Stuck! Really? Her feet in the air? That's a riot!" As soon as Claire laughed, Lester saw it as funny. When Lester laughed, Alfred as a matter of course did the same. Myron was taken aback for a moment, but then he, too, was struck and joined them.

"Tell me another story," begged Claire.

"I know one," spoke up Alfred. What a surprise. He was usually absolutely quiet, a presence more than a personality. He simply *was* in the world. His simplicity had a stillness to it in the way of a stone or a tree, without tension, without friction. "I know a good one," he said. "I learned it by heart in school." Almost unable to contain himself, he began. "On a dark and stormy night, on the banks of a beautiful shore, stood a captain and his forty men. 'Do you want me to tell you a story?' said the captain. 'Yes!' said the forty men. 'Well,' said the captain . . . .'" Alfred could hardly go on. Stumbling with laughter, he continued, " 'Well, it was a dark and stormy night, on the banks of a beautiful shore. In a cave stood a captain and his forty men. "Do you want me to tell you a story?" said the captain. "Yes!" said the forty men. "Well, it was a dark and stormy night . . . ." ' "

He would have gone on and on, but Claire put her hand over his mouth. "Unlearn that immediately!" she ordered, tickling him.

One night, after much talk, it was decided that what they had to do was to go to Prospect Park to look at the rowboats. Myron told them that at the big lake in the park the boats were for rent by the hour. He wanted to check how the passenger seats were put in. Naturally, he needed a passenger seat since they were all going to take rides with him the very day the boat was launched.

It was decided that Saturday they were all going to take a picnic lunch and visit the rowboats in the park. Lester was beside himself, longing to go, afraid to go. He had never been on an excursion before with people his own age, only with his mother. He knew he would have trouble convincing her and so he did.

"Without me?" she exclaimed, incredulous. "Lester,

you might fall, you might get lost, anything could happen. Better I come with you."

That did it. Lester told the others he couldn't go.

"Don't be silly," said Claire. "We'll talk to her. She'll let you, you'll see. I'll be, oh so nicey-nice." She minced across the floor of the paint room, fluttering her hands and batting her eyes. "And Myron here will wash his neck, right, My?" Myron shied a piece of wood at her. Claire said seriously, "I'll tell her I'm a famous brain surgeon and Myron here is a registered nurse, so you'll be in good hands. How's that?"

Lester groaned.

Mrs. Klopper consented easily when Myron and Claire went to talk to her. Despite her misgivings, it was the words "picnic" and "outing" and "together" that made it so tempting, so beautifully ordinary. Besides, she was dazzled by the fact that a girl was going, too. Even such a girl as Claire. "That's a girl?" she sniffed. "Tsk, tsk, poor thing. Wearing boys' *shmatahs* yet." Luckily, Claire didn't hear her favorite shorts referred to as rags. She had dressed up for the visit.

Mrs. Burt was delighted that Alfred was going along. "You see? He's liked. He has friends, he's going to be all right!" she told her husband, buoyant and persuaded.

That Saturday they met downstairs in front of Lester's house because it was on the way to the station. Each carried a bag of sandwiches and some money for drinks and carfare. It was a perfect day for the outing, clear and sunny, not too hot. Lester looked across the street at the schoolyard full of bustle and play. He remembered his afternoon walks with his mother along the wire fence and felt a million years away from what he was then. He gave Alfie's hand a squeeze as the four of them set off for the station.

It was slow going for the long blocks to the elevated train. Then they had to climb a long flight of steps. Their nickels deposited, they waited on the outdoor platform for their train to Prospect Park. Alfred knew exactly how many stops the train would make.

They were left off right at the park, a big leafy area in the heart of Brooklyn. Wide cement paths, bordered by benches, wove and branched like lines drawn at random on a page. They would have gotten thoroughly lost if they hadn't seen a sign, "To the Boathouse" and an arrow pointing the way.

The little band made a curious sight as they walked along. Lester and Alfie held hands, separated only when Alfred had to examine a cigarette pack for tin foil or pick up a discarded matchcover to add to his collection. Myron and Claire, walking in front, had to stop often to wait for them to catch up. They were so used to Lester and Alfred they were unconscious of the interest of the bench-sitters. Besides, they were not without interest themselves, Claire looking like a girl in drag and Myron a beefy shepherd of a peculiar flock.

They finally reached the boathouse, which bordered the long meandering lake. The large, covered pavilion had a fleet of rowboats to one side, lined up like school-children waiting to be taken out to play. A few steps down from the boathouse was a boardwalk where the boats were tied. The boats, all painted the same bilious green, were heavy, ugly, flatbottomed things at rest. Like swans, they had grace only in motion.

They stepped down the few steps to the wooden pier and walked out to the very last boat in the row. Myron stared down at it. "Well, it's different from mine," he conceded.

"Yours is more symmetrical," offered Lester, which was a loyal way of saying that there was not much difference between the front and the back of Myron's boat. This was a sore point because, try as he might, Myron could not get the wood to bend so he could get the proper point. They all decided it didn't matter; he wasn't out to win either a race or a beauty contest.

While the rest of them kept watch for the boatman, Myron climbed into one of the boats to examine it more closely. He studied the seating arrangements and then looked at the oars.

He sat down so suddenly the boat slapped the water. He looked dumbfounded, as if the oar had spoken to him. He turned sharply to the other three, who were watching silently from the wooden walk.

"Looka here! I forgot something. What a dope I am!" He was pointing to the oarlock, a U-shaped metal piece with a tail at the closed end that fitted neatly into a hole in the side of the boat. The oar rested on it like an arm resting on a slingshot. Without it holding the oar in place, rowing would be difficult, not to say impossible.

"What is it? What did you forget?"

"These things here." He slipped one out of the hole and held it up. They could see how necessary it was. He slipped the other oar out of the oarlock and then held both metal objects clutched to him as if they were the family jewels. A terrible impulse was taking hold of him. He wanted those oarlocks desperately. He needed them. Should he? No, yes . . . .

His temptation was obvious. Claire said urgently, "Grab them, Myron. Go on, take them." She couldn't bear the look on Myron's face.

As if she were the voice of conscience giving him permission, he thrust them inside his shirt and scrambled out of the boat.

Too late. The boatman was waiting on the steps for them, watching them. He stood with his legs apart, thick-necked and unshaven. He was a shaggy sentry barring their way. His eyes were the muddy gray of the lake and as cold. He said, "What do you think you're doing? Hand them over, kid, or I'll call the police."

They were all of them terrified. Myron silently handed the oarlocks to the man, whose hand was outstretched. He looked the four of them over contemptuously, almost amused. "Now get out of here and don't let me see you around these boats again." He was enjoying their terror.

They found a picnic bench and ate their lunch in silence. The incident had shaken them. Only Alfred retained his pleasure in the outing; the park was a treasure trove of litter. Lunch finished, they pooled their money and had just enough to share a hot dog and orange drink from the cart with the big orange and black umbrella.

It was time to head for home.

"Which way?" asked Claire.

Myron looked around. He had no idea. Neither did Alfred because he had been walking with his head down, not noticing where they were going. Myron chose a way. They walked along the path for a while, seeing nothing familiar.

"We ought to go back to the boathouse and start from there," suggested Claire, knowing that they could wander around aimlessly for hours.

Myron wouldn't hear of it. He didn't want to see that boathouse again for the next million years. They followed one path for a while, branched off to another and soon knew they were lost.

"Let's ask someone," said Claire.

Up ahead were a group of boys and girls hanging around the water fountain, horsing around. They were pushing, screaming, scrambling to get a controlling thumb on the fountain, squirting one another, paying no attention to anyone but themselves.

"Maybe they know the way to the station. Let's ask them." said Claire.

Myron stared at the scene and hurriedly said, "No, no, we'll find it."

Claire sent him a scathing look. "Really, Myron, you're the limit sometimes."

She walked up alone to the fountain while the others gaped. Myron felt the sweat start as she pulled at one of the group for attention. She spoke, pointed back at them, listened, nodded, smiled and returned. No trouble at all.

"Let's go," was all she said.

Again silence until they were on the station platform waiting for their train. Myron didn't know quite how to put it. "How did you do that, Claire? I mean, have the nerve and all?"

"Do what? What nerve?"

"Those kids back there. Don't you get nervous? About talking to people, I mean. Think they will laugh at you or something?"

He could almost feel how his face would burn and his shoulders feel all prickly with embarrassment. The words would stick and he could always tell people were ready to laugh at him.

"Yeah, sure, sometimes I guess." She bent over the platform looking down the black tunnel for signs of their train. The station was deserted that time of day, dingy and airless. Their voices echoed in the dim cavern.

Lester listened in amazement. So Myron was shy and self-conscious with strangers, too. He, Lester, with his good reason, wasn't the only one. And Claire also? He never would have thought that.

Alfred was wandering around, poking into the trash cans. Myron called him back; the train might come any minute. "Are you sure you know which train we get on?" he asked him.

"Sure I know," said Alfred, joining them at one of the steel beams that lined the platform. "It says Brighton Beach on it." He tapped Lester on the shoulder. "That's for nothin'," he said, and laughed at his joke and took Lester's hand again.

Myron returned to his question, irritated with himself and Claire, too. "But you went over to those kids anyway?" he persisted.

"Myron, I just used my Aziff Theory. That's what I do."

"What's that? Something you learned in algebra?"

"Huh, algebra. Very funny. Wait'll I tell Mr. Pargot."

"Who's he?"

"Mr. Pargot, my track coach? He says in a race if you show that you're nervous, you're dead."

Alfred shook his head at this. Solemnly he said, "Gee whizz, dead." He didn't know running was so dangerous.

Myron was lost. "So what has that got to do with . . . what you did? That Aziff stuff?"

Claire stood on one foot. The other, bent at the knee, rested on the pillar behind her. Her gray eyes were intent, her restless body quiet for a change as she spoke.

"So Mr. Pargot says if you act as if you're sure of yourself, you know, confident, then people will think you are. He says people see what you are by the way you act, not by the way you feel inside. You can act *as if* . . . anything you want. And pretty soon the way you are on the outside becomes the way you feel on the inside. Get it? Aziff? So . . . I'm working on it. I bet those kids at the fountain didn't know how I really felt. . . ."

Her last words were drowned out by the train screeching into the station.

Myron didn't get it. But all the ride home Lester felt full of protest. Wasn't that just what he hated? People judging you by your front? Wasn't he a good example of that?

He said as much on the way home. It confused Claire, but then she told him her Aziff Theory must be for bad things about yourself you wanted to change.

"Even you could do with some change, Lester," she said drily.

Getting off the train, Lester watched Myron walking dejectedly in front of them. The Aziff Theory could wait. He knew Myron was thinking of those oarlocks, wanting them, yearning for them. The shock of an idea coursed through him. An idea so daring it stopped his breath. He and Alfred had collected wood for the boat. But they were going to do something else, something much harder. He and Alfred were going to steal those oarlocks for Myron.

Chapter Nine

Something awful was happening to Alfred.

"Alfred! Alfred! Oh, dear God, look at him! Alfred, what's the matter with you?"

The family was standing in the hallway under the big clock, just returned from a day in the country. Alfred had been quiet on the drive home, but there was nothing unusual about that. He loved just riding along, looking out the window. Once in the house, they hadn't even put down the shopping bags full of corn and tomatoes, the summer treats of the countryside, when his mother noticed that Alfred was looking . . . well, there was no way to describe it, she cried later. He had turned a sick gray under his tan, drained of color as if blood had fled his body. His eyes were open, unfocused and unseeing, his mouth working. In and out, in and out, his lips pursed as if concentrating on some deep problem. His hand, his bad hand, began to tremble and then to vibrate in small movements. He heard nothing, not his mother's cries, not his father's cries, as if listening to some exquisite workings deep inside his body took all his attention, needed his life's blood, sapped his soul.

Then . . . it released him. He slumped against his mother, eyes closed, body limp, unconscious. Her arms wrapped around him, supporting him, his head on her breast. She lifted her head and cried out, "He's gone! He's dead!"

At this cry, Richy, who had been shrinking against the fish tank, scurried into the bedroom . . . not to see, not to hear, not to know, unable to bear any of it.

But Alfred wasn't dead. His father carried him to the sofa, and his color began to return. Soon he opened his eyes and smiled at the faces above. He sat up and said he guessed he was sleepy. He said it slower than usual, as if slightly drugged, but otherwise himself again. His mother and father exchanged a deep look in which bewilderment and relief and fear merged to become a new expression, minted that very moment.

Over and over they asked him, was he all right? How did he feel? Never in all his life a complainer about anything, it didn't mean much to them when he said he felt fine. But they could see with their own eyes that he was. But then, what had happened to him? Alfred didn't remember a thing, only coming home and then waking up on the sofa. He couldn't tell them anything except that he felt fine. He couldn't understand why they looked so anxious and asked him those questions. No, he didn't want anything to eat. He was still full from supper and he was sleepy. He wanted to go to bed. Nothing unusual in that, either.

It was as if it had never happened at all. As if it were some bad dream they had shared.

Later that night, after the boys were in bed, Alfred's

mother and father sat in the kitchen drinking coffee. They were both worn out, but they needed to talk, to go over that scene again and again.

"What do we do now, Lou?" Her voice quivered. Exhausted from the day, she felt overwhelmed, unable to face some new and terrible fact about her afflicted son.

Mr. Burt stirred his coffee, lining up his thoughts, trying to decide what was best for them all. It was quiet in the kitchen. Sounds of plumbing ran through the building, feet thumped upstairs, but they didn't hear it. The hall clock chimed the hour, its melody sweetening the air. What had happened to Alfred seemed so unreal to them. There they were, sitting having their coffee as they had done so many times, the boys safe in bed, everything as usual.

It was the usualness of it all. That, and the terrible need to believe all was as usual, that decided Alfred's father. He pushed back his cup and saucer, and leaning towards her on his forearms, he said, "There's nothing to do, honey. I don't think we should do anything but wait and see. Maybe this will never happen again, maybe it's just some freak thing that will never be repeated, whatever it is. Look, if it happens again we'll take him to the best doctor we can find and we'll go on from there." He sighed. "But for now, Flo, well, let's just wait and see. Don't forget, we just got back from a big day at the lake. Maybe the boy was just overtired."

"Yes, yes!" Mrs. Burt eagerly agreed, her face brightening with every word. "Of *course*! Alfred was *over*tired. Of course it must be that. Oh, I'm sure of it!"

Mr. Burt watched her, filled with love and pity for her,

for her eagerness to accept an easy explanation, even if it wasn't convincing.

She kept chattering on, almost cheerful again.

"Remember when we were going out in that canoe this afternoon? Remember how Alfie looked at the boat and asked where the oarlocks were?" She laughed at this. "Now how did he know about oarlocks? The little dickens! That's pretty smart to know about those things, don't you think that's smart?"

Her husband shook his head and laughed with her. "And when I explained that oarlocks were for rowboats and not canoes, he said he knew that, and that the boat downstairs that he, get that, he said *he* was building, was much nicer than a canoe. Have you seen the boat they are building in the basement, honey?"

No, she hadn't seen it, but wasn't it wonderful that he had friends now. "They must like him. They maybe can see how good and sweet he is, don't you think? Of course, poor Lester is worse off than Alfie. Much. I think Alfie is smarter than he is, too. I haven't heard him ever say a word, have you?"

Now she was almost gay. The nightmare of the early evening receded like the tide. Her boy was safe, nothing was the matter, and he was smarter and much better off than others she could name. She stood up, gathered the few dishes and brought them to the sink. She stood there a long moment, her back to her husband, looking down into the sink.

There was something about the set of her body that made her husband, watching her every movement, brace himself.

She turned to him and said very quietly, "We can't afford more doctors, can we."

It was a statement, not a question.

"We can afford anything we have to afford, Flo."

"Don't let them put him away. He's not sick enough for that." She leaped to her deepest fear.

"Nobody's going to put him away, Flo. Why would you think that?"

He, too, stood up. He took her hand and swung it back and forth in some private semaphore of their very own.

"C'mon, let's go to bed."

They smiled a weary smile at one another.

Chapter Ten

Today's the day! Today's the day we steal the oarlocks! God, I feel as if I haven't slept for a year. Well, I can sleep anytime. How often in my life have I planned a heist? Come to think of it, how often in my life have I planned anything at all? No wonder She has said to me at least a dozen times these past few days, "What's the matter with you, Lester? You're all wound up? Are you feeling all right?" One of her strings—the one attached to my mind—isn't working. She pulls on it and it comes loose. Nothing caught on the other end. Well, better for her this way. Suppose she pulls and I say, "Ma, I'm a little tense these days because Alfred and I, the two sorry Charlies, are about to pull off a heist in the park. Look for me in the newspapers." Can't you hear the explosion? Europe will think a war has started. No, I tell her nothing. She ought to thank me for it.

I told Alfie yesterday that we are going to the park today. But I didn't tell him what for. There's no use telling him to keep his mouth shut about anything. What goes in his ears runs out of his mouth like pouring water through a funnel.

I told him when we were going around the neighborhood as usual, pulling the wagon and looking for wood. I said to him, "Alfie, let's go to the park again tomorrow instead of looking for wood." His face lit up and he grinned as I knew he would and he said, "Can we look at the boats again?" Just what I wanted. Then he said, "I'll hafta ask my mother."

Well I knew I would have to go with him when he asked her. I told my own mother we were all going to the park again. But maybe Mrs. Burt wouldn't check with Ma. Maybe she would call Myron. And the last thing I wanted was that. We are going alone. Not with Claire, not with Myron. Just the two of us.

We headed back to his house and on the way Alfie spotted a really good piece of wood lying in the strip of grass that runs along the apartment building. The grass strip is only about three feet wide, but it is fenced in by iron spikes, looking like little spears. Believe me, I give that fence a wide berth. One misstep and I'd be nailed—a little dead Jesus. You would think that strip of anemic grass was an estate and the iron spears were to keep the poachers from bagging the wildlife. Robin Hood might roam again here in Brooklyn, so let's put up the spears to keep him out.

Well, there was that beautiful piece of wood. How to get it? Alfie bent over and tried to reach it from outside. Nothing doing. I told him to come away, never mind. But sometimes he gets an idea in his head, it's hard to budge him. I watched in horror as he climbed over those wicked spears. Of course the fence isn't high, just up to my knees actually. But he could get awfully hurt if he fell. One slip and there's an arrow through him!

But he doesn't fall. And so another concern of mine is laid to rest. I knew Alfie, not me, was the one who would have to climb into the boat for the oarlocks, and now I could see that he'd be able to do it, I hope, I hope.

We put the long piece of wood away in the paint room and went upstairs to the third floor to call on Alfred's mother.

I told her that we're going to the park again tomorrow —was that okay? It was about the longest sentence I ever spoke to her. Actually, in my mind I don't speak much to her either. I just say over and over, "I love you," while she pats my head. Maybe it was my imagination, but I thought I saw a flash of something new in her eyes. She hesitated just a bit. The last time we went to the park she was absolutely delighted. Now her eyes had a glint of . . . fear maybe? I could see her shake this off and say as warmly as ever, "Of course. How nice for Alfred that all of you are going again."

I know you can lie by *not* saying something just as much as you can by saying. So I lied. I let her think we are all going, not just the two of us.

She wanted me to stay, to have supper with them. "I'll call your mother," she said. "If it's all right with her, we'd love to have you. It doesn't get dark till late . . . . no, no, we'll see you home no matter what." She smiled at me. She was eager, I could tell. Eager for Alfie's sake. And I was tempted—for my own sake. But I didn't want to risk any more questions. So I made my excuses.

I told Alfie that I would meet him downstairs about eleven and to bring lunch. Could he bring it in a shopping bag? That way we would have a place to put all the stuff he'd collect. He could? Fine. I could see him already, dreaming of tin foil. Good. A shopping bag is part of my plan.

So when I wake up this morning and see that the day is gray, overcast, and smell the strong ocean smell, I say to myself, uh oh. I know what that means. It can't rain! It just must not rain.

I fret the morning away, looking out of the window every few minutes. Finally, it's time to go. Alfred is waiting for me, carrying his shopping bag. I have mine. The shopping bags are for the oarlocks of course, a double bag, sure to hold them. Mrs. Burt leans out of her window upstairs and calls down, "Are you sure it won't rain?" What kind of question is that? Today I'm God so I won't let it rain? I look up at her and shake my head no. Meaning no, I'm not sure. She takes it the other way of course and waves and pulls her head back inside.

I'm terribly anxious to be off, afraid that any moment Myron or Claire will appear and ask us where we are going. It's the surprise I'm after—my present to Myron, to the both of them. All I can think of is the look on their faces when we hand them the oarlocks and they see what we have done—by ourselves. Surprise, oh yes, and disbelief and respect. Oh my yes, the respect! "What?! You mean to say that you, that you had the guts, the nerve . . . . Why, this is the best . . . Lester, you're terrific!" And on and on. Talk about dreams of glory. No ten-year-old could match me. I'n sure no normal person my age could be this childish.

On the way to the station, we pass the movie house

with long lines of kids waiting to get in. My heart sinks. Movies equal rain.

Once we get out at Prospect Park I feel better about the weather since, as they say, no rain is good rain. But now my stomach is starting to tango. "Oh, dear God," I pray, "You won't let Your poor little crippled children get arrested today, will You?" God and I have had rather stand-off relations, you might say. Way off. I don't appreciate His sense of humor is the thing. But right now I would knock on wood and kiss a rabbit's foot if I had one. I would kiss a pig's ass if I thought it would bring us luck. I would even pray.

Alfred leads us right to the lake as I knew he would. And there are the boats waiting for us, offering up their oarlocks like girls in the movies saying, "Take me, I'm yours."

I look around for the boatman. Not in sight. I look through the window inside the pavilion and there he is, feet up on a table, riffling through a magazine. Because of the rotten day there aren't even people around. Unbelievable! I kept myself awake for nights planning what to do under cover of crowds, and now there's no one. The cloudy day was the luckiest thing that could have happened.

Now here's the touchy part. I tell Alfred that I want him to get in a boat and slip out the oarlocks and give them to me. We are going to bring them to Myron as a surprise.

He looks at me, his dark eyes troubled, trying to figure something out. I don't mention the word steal, I don't tell him he has to be quiet, or to hurry, or anything. I don't want to worry him at all. He just says, "It's all right to do that?" As firmly as I can, I say yes, go ahead. He believes me. Trusts me. I'm working very hard on myself not to get the jangles. I *must* stay in control.

Now what happens next is the damndest thing. I can't believe it myself. Are we invisible or what? As if a charmed cloud surrounds us, Alfred lowers himself inside the boat and manages to slip one oarlock off and then the other. No trouble at all. He hands them to me one at a time and I put them in his shopping bag. Any second I expect a voice to shout at us, but no one does. No one sees us.

Alfred gets out, picks up his bag and we just walk away. Just like that.

I tell you such a rush of triumph shoots through me I feel that it shouts aloud. I want to run or dance or do whatever other people do when they are feeling so great. I feel as if I have shaken a fist at life.

We get to a tree and lean against it. I hug Alfie to me and we grin at one another.

Then I see the boatman, the rough guy who chased us last Saturday, come out of the boathouse, look up at the overcast sky and then at his boats. Is he going to check them?

I don't wait to find out. If I can see him, he can see us. We get out of there fast. By fast I mean like two turtles climbing uphill. I say "Hurry!" to Alfie, but he's not worrying about stolen goods or police or jail. He still has to stop and investigate papers under a bench or look inside the trash cans. We aren't going fast enough. Any moment I expect to feel a heavy hand on my shoulder and the oarlocks discovered. Suddenly it is all too much for me. My legs buckle and I fall.

I feel myself being picked up. And when I get a look at who is helping me to my feet I nearly fall again. Some weird guy is brushing me off. Is he for real? Dressed up like that? He looks like he's about to be married. Maybe he's the bride. He's all in white, head to toe, hat, vest, suit and shoes, like some cuckoo snowflake. Hiding his neck like a scarf is a funny striped tie with a pearl stickpin. He even has a flower in his buttonhole, a red one that just about matches his big nose. Black pointy moustaches move as he speaks. But what kind of voice is this? It sounds as if he is belching instead of talking. As he brushes me off, he asks, "Are you all right, sonny?" I can understand him, but barely. I never heard anything like it.

I didn't notice at first that there is someone with him. She's a motherly looking woman, plain clothes, no makeup at all, hair pulled back in a comfortable bun and kind, kind eyes. He's the peacock and she's the sparrow. She repeats what the old guy said, asks me if I'm all right.

Well, I am and then again I'm not. I can't get out a word, my tongue and my heart all tied up with the bag of oarlocks Alfred is carrying. He is standing by, just watching, and the woman has him by the hand.

The next thing I know is they have me sitting on a bench. I catch my breath and smile up at them. I manage to say, "Okay."

Then they walk us behind the bushes and there on the grass is a small table with a picnic lunch on it. The table is covered by a white cloth and in the center sits a vase with a flower sticking out of it. It's like some magazine advertisement. The table looks as dressed up as the old guy. Twins you might say.

"We come here every fine day, don't we Frankie?" says the lady and she tells us there's plenty to eat and we should sit down and share their picnic. Fine day, she says. I look at the gray sky and think they're both nutty. Friendly but nutty. They sit on a couple of folding chairs at the table and we sit on the grass and they hand us things. No baloney sandwiches for us today. We are given chicken sandwiches, all sliced white meat the way I like it and with the crusts cut off. Then, from a pail sitting beside the man is pulled a bottle of wine. I saw the pail right away, but for all I know he was going to dig in the sandbox with it. Play patty-cakes. We are handed a glass of wine. Alfie takes one sip and spits it out.

"Sour!" he says and makes a face.

I think so, too. But it seems so elegant to me to be sipping wine just like a character in a book, I sip anyway. I can't believe any of this is happening. One minute I'm about to die of fright and the next I'm drinking wine, having a party with a couple of screwballs. I feel perfectly safe from the boatman, behind these bushes, and I give myself over to the entertainment. And that is just what these two are doing—entertaining us as if they were on a stage and we are the audience. It turns out that is just what they once were, on the stage doing vaudeville acts. At least, they were on the stage "until Frankie had his operation," says the lady, looking at him as if she would gladly pay admission to see him anytime. She called him Frankie and her name is Myrt or Sweetheart and between the two of them they had some little act going: He tells the jokes in his no-voice and she does the laughing.

"A man goes to a head doctor. 'Doctor,' he says, 'I'm a fish. I can live in water.' Doctor says, 'If you can do that you're a miracle.' 'No Doctor, I'm not a miracle,' says the man, 'I'm a mackerel.'"

Frankie laughs soundlessly, lifts up his straw hat and wipes his bald head with a cloth napkin. She wipes tears of laughter from her eyes and says, "Oh Frankie, you're a caution. You did that joke first at the Pantages Theater in Milwaukee. No, no." She covers her mouth with her hand, "I tell a fib! It was at the Geary in San Francisco, wasn't it?" Frankie nods.

I bet she's heard that joke a thousand times. Frankie looks over at us and says to Alfie mainly, "A mackerel is a kind of fish, you know."

Alfie says, "Oh yeah, a kind of fish." He didn't get it at all but Frankie and Sweetheart smile at him as if he had said something brilliant.

Then, while Alfie and I feed bits of bread to the birds, they do some kind of act for us. They come out from the bushes, doing a dance step. He first and then she, both pretending to be playing an instrument. I think it's a flute he's playing and she's strumming away on a guitar I guess it's supposed to be, and she's singing a song. You can tell he thinks his playing is teriffic. Well, they dance along and then she sings, oh, a terrible note, way off key. And he stops and looks at her like he's going to kill and they go back and start again. Same thing happens. At the same place, she louses it up. It really is funny the way he looks at her. Alfie's practically rolling on the grass. Well, this one time when they do it again we all expect her to do it wrong at the same place. Frankie stops playing and waits. We wait for it, too. But no! She sings it perfectly and goes right on past him and across the stage. Oh, his face when she did that! You could tell he was a good actor. And she, too.

We clap as hard as we can and they take lots of bows. I don't know who's having a better time, them or us. They never ask a question, don't try to find out anything about us, why we are in the park, where we are going or coming from. They just take us as if we were dropped from the sky as their afternoon treat.

When they sit down again, I get up the nerve to ask something I wanted to know ever since I heard Frankie talk.

"Did that operation have something to do with your voice?"

Frankie looks at me, amused. Then he gulps some air and in this hollow way says, "Yep. Took out my voice box. Now I swallow air to speak. I'm good at it. See?"

He swallows air and forms words with the belch. Terrific! I'm going to try that sometime. He's really proud, you can see that.

I say something stupid like, "I'm sorry."

He just nods and says, "Hell, everyone has something or other. Sometimes it shows, sometimes not." He winks at us.

All of a sudden I think of Claire and I see what she means. Here's her Aziff Theory in person. Here's this old guy not a bit sorry for himself. Or at least acting as if he isn't. And so no one else feels sorry for him either. The opposite. He could be crying in his wine over himself. Instead, he's giving life a good kick in the pants. And, it flashes in my mind, and not stealing oarlocks to do it either! Wow.

Myrt sees me staring into space and says very gently, "Well, I guess you two boys want to get along."

She's been so nice. She's fine. And so is Frankie. They don't offer to shake hands as so many people do, embarrassing the life out of me, knowing that they have to make a grab for my hand as it goes by. No, they just say good-by and we all thank one another and smile a lot. They tell us the way to the station.

Alfie picks up the bag of oarlocks and we leave Frankie and Myrt sitting at their table.

Chapter Eleven

The two boys walked to the station in silence, completely unaware of the picture they made as they followed the broad leafy paths of the park to the exit. Alfred limping, one arm drawn up, hand dangling, the other arm weighed down by a large shopping bag. One leg of his knickers had come undone and flapped as he dragged his foot along. His white cotton shirt, so carefully pressed by his mother that morning, was stained by grass and food. It had parted company from the knickers, seeking the freedom to stretch and spread so that it appeared as if his clothes were far too large for his small wiry body. He was pulled to one side by the weight of the oarlocks, making him look even shorter, his black curls bobbing just below Lester's shoulder.

Lester tottered beside him, neat and tidy, but unsteady as a drunk. His fine features and fair skin and hair rose above Alfred's darkness like a study in contrasts: day to night, high to low. Even the way they walked was utterly unmatched, unrhythmic, as if they each stepped to their own random music.

The day had cleared and the park, a green haven in the busy cement of Brooklyn, was now filled with bench-sitters, carriage pushers, strolling couples and the perpetual motion of playing children. The boys left a trail of head shaking, of grunts of pity, of morbid curiosity in their wake. "Poor things, poor things," was written on the faces of those who noticed them go by, if not said aloud.

The "poor things" were drenched with delight over the adventure of the afternoon. Every once in a while Lester would catch Alfie's eye and then the both of them would break into grins. Or else it was Alfred who nudged Lester and then the two of them would burst into laughter. They had only to look at one another for complete understanding. Just that, that feeling of understanding without words, was yet another new experience for them. The secret sharing, the unity of it, made Lester realize how isolated he had once been. How dry life was without a friend to share it.

He suddenly longed to be home in his room. He longed for the night to cover him so he could take out the events of the day and look at them one by one, as he long ago poured over his baseball cards. Sometimes he felt he really lived events in his life more deeply when he was alone to think about them than when they were actually happening. He felt as if a light bulb had gone off over his head like in the funny papers. New thoughts, glimpses of new possibilities, shadowed the edges of his mind. He needed time and quiet to explore them. He thought of Frankie, so jaunty and undaunted. Of course he was old and maybe things don't matter so much to you when you're old. But if only he could be more like that funny man. If only he didn't expect failure all the time. He remembered his mother telling him that he hid, that he didn't give "them" a chance. Them. The word turned his thoughts bitter. It stood for all those people who judged only by the outside of things, all who didn't look beyond his body to the person he was inside. Then Claire's Aziff Theory and Frankie flooded his mind again, the light bulb showing that maybe he could change the way he was, too.

He pushed those thoughts away for later. Now they were at the station. They each deposited a nickel in the slot and went through the turnstile to the platform to wait for their train. Lester led the way to a bench along the grimy tiled wall. They sat. Alfred shook his head back and forth, back and forth, saying, "Boy, oh boy, boyoh-boy," in rhythm to the wagging.

Then he said, "They were some chicken sandwiches, hey Les?"

"The best. And you didn't drink the wine!"

"Naw. It was sour." He grimaced at the memory. "I like ginger ale better, don't you?"

"Yeah, but I like the idea of drinking wine. I didn't drink much though. I just sipped. Say, ever see anyone dressed up like that Frankie?"

They laughed together.

"Nope. But I liked the flower. I never saw a man wear a flower before. Say Les, why did he talk so funny?"

"Didn't you hear him say? He had an operation?"

"Oh. Oh . . . gee whizz, an operation." He was sobered at this news.

"Now he doesn't have a voice, see? He has to belch

and then talk. I don't know how he does it. I can't belch unless I have to. Can you?"

"Yeah, sometimes. But my mother sends me away from the table when I do that."

Another idea made Alfred laugh again. "It was like a show, wasn't it, Les? With them two? Wasn't it like a show? I'm going to tell my mother we saw a show this afternoon and we got a present for Myron."

"Jesus, the oarlocks!" Lester had forgotten them. "Here, let me see them."

Alfred bent and fished around in the shopping bag at his feet. He pulled them out and placed them in his lap. They both stared at them for a while.

"Hey Les, what's this thing here sticking down like that?"

"This part here? That's a tail piece. Myron will drill a hole in the side of the boat and this part will fit down into it. Then you put the oar on this round part and it holds it in place, see?" The realization that they were actually looking at the oarlocks, that they had done it, pulled it off, overcame him. Lester cried, "Wow! Can you see their faces when we give this to them? Can't you see Myron when he gets these oarlocks?"

"He'll be glad, huh? Myron will be glad when he gets this present from us. Wait till I tell my mother. . . ."

A train thundered into the station. The two boys looked up, watching the windows flash by until the train came to a stop.

"Is that our train, Alfie?"

Alfred knew. "Naw. That's the local. We want the express."

They waited until the doors closed and the train pulled out. Once again it was quiet in the station.

Lester remembered what Alfred was about to say before the train came. "Alfie, I'm going to ask you a favor. Do you have to tell your mother about these oarlocks? I mean, you don't have to tell your mother everything."

"You mean I shouldn't tell her?" His dark eyes turned on Lester as if the sight would help him understand such an idea.

"I want it to be a secret. You know, just between the two of us."

"Oh, a secret!" That he understood. "I can keep a secret, Les. Sure I can keep a secret." An important assignment had just been given him. He was ready for it.

Another train rumbled into the station and this time the boys picked up the shopping bag and boarded. They sat on the worn cane seats closest to the doors. The train began to move and Lester fell to reading the advertisements marching along the walls of the train like an open magazine. Each one got his close attention. He would read anything, ketchup bottles, cereal boxes, telephone books if there was nothing else handy.

The train was fairly empty, only a few shoppers returning from the "City" as Manhattan was called, or salesmen with battered brief cases between their legs. A drunk was hanging on the white pole near them. It was too early for rush hour.

The train emerged to the open air, running along an elevated track so that Lester caught glimpses of the insides of people's apartments. Living statues flipped by:

a man at a kitchen table, a cup raised to his lips, a woman with a hairbrush, an old lady with a hand raised in some forever uncompleted gesture. It was like seeing candid snapshots in an album.

The train stopped. A few more people came in, a few left. Lester craned to see what station it was. The big sign on the platform said "Kings Highway." He turned to Alfred to make sure theirs was the next stop.

The words died in his throat. His heart moved and sickened him. Something was terribly wrong with Alfred. He was ashen, a dead color. He was unseeing, although his eyes were open. His lips were working in and out, in and out. His one hand, the crippled hand, had a life of its own, shaking rapidly, making wider and wider arcs.

Lester was transfixed with horror, managing only to mouth Alfred's name, not knowing, having no idea at all what was happening to his friend. But Alfred was far, far beyond the reach of the voice of a friend.

The train hurtled on, but time stood still for Lester. Forever he was locked in that moment, Alfie beset, and he watching, helpless and terrified.

Then it all changed. Alfred slumped against Lester as if the giant hand that had him in its grip had finished some awful business and had tossed him away like garbage.

The train slowed. They were coming in to their station. Lester had an arm about Alfred, supporting him. Alfred's head drooped, his body limp, totally out of it, unconscious.

Lester looked about him wildly. He tried to call "Help!" but what came out of his strangled throat was hardly that. The train was stopping. When the doors opened they had to get off, and fast, before the doors closed again. There were faces in the train, people with two hands and steady legs, people able to see his predicament and able to come to his aid. No one moved. He tried to get to his feet, pulling Alfred up at the same time. He raised them both an inch or so and collapsed back on the seat. Again he tried to cry the word "Help!"

A woman alone, one of the shoppers with packages wrapped in fancy paper on her lap, called out an accusation, her voice frightened, full of loathing. "You should be ashamed taking a sick boy like that on a train!" She looked down, she looked away, her eyes seeking anything but what was before her. The drunk swung around the pole in a daze of his own. Others in the car, living whole people, men and women grown, turned their faces away, avoiding the sight, wanting no part of something terrible and beyond them. They weren't involved and maybe if they didn't look, it would all go away by itself.

The doors opened. There was no time. No time for thinking what to do, so Lester did what he had to. Never could he recall those moments. Never could he tell just what he did. From some untapped place, he found the strength to pull Alfred through the doors before they closed.

Alfred lay on the cement platform and Lester collapsed beside him. Suddenly, concerned hands were there to help them both. An ambulance was called. Alfred was taken away and Lester was driven home.

Chapter Twelve

Lester sank into his bed and into sleep. Sometime during the night he got up to lock his door. The next day he refused to come out, no matter how much his mother carried on. All day she had knocked and begged, threatened, tempted with food or predicted her own early demise at his hands. Nothing had opened that door to her. By evening she was at her wit's end.

When her husband came home, her greeting was, "All day long he's been in his room, that boy. Not a thing to eat all day!" She stood before him, drying her hands on her apron, supper smells rising from her. "He won't talk to me! He won't let me in!" Distraught, she looked for someone, something to blame. "I knew he shouldn't have anything to do with that Alfred. I feel sorry for that boy and I hope he doesn't have anything bad, but I warned Lester. I warned, and this is what I get. Manny, do something!"

Lester's father hadn't said a word through all this. He slowly took off his hat and opened the hall closet to hang it carefully in its place. The evening paper was under his

94

arm and he offered it to her, as he did every night. It was as if she hadn't spoken.

She looked at the paper and then at him. She wheeled around and ran down the hall to Lester's room. She slapped the closed door as if it were the source of her troubles. "Lester, come out of there. Your father is home. Supper is on the table. Enough already, you hear me?"

From behind the door Lester said, "The strings are gone, Ma. Leave me alone."

"See? He's talking crazy. Strings he says." She slapped the door again.

Mr. Klopper came up beside her and took her hand from the door. "Take it easy, Mae. You're getting yourself in an uproar. He'll come out when he's hungry enough."

She didn't look at him. She talked to the door, her voice bitter. "Sure, and by that time I'll be dead. But what do you care? What do you know?" Now her day of worry and frustration opened gates. "You know from nothing about your son. Your own son and what do you know? You're out all the time. Always out!"

At this, Mr. Klopper seemed to swell, anger filling him up, filling up the hallway. He seemed to grow larger, heavier. He raised his hand as if to strike her, but ran it over his bald head instead.

"Out all the time, am I?" he roared. "Sure I'm out. And you know why, Mae? You know why I'm out? Because you pushed me out. You chose *him*, not me. Not even to share. I'm out because there's no room for me here." He pushed at her shoulder. "Get away from that door."

She threw him a wild look and ran into their bedroom.

Mr. Klopper knocked on Lester's door and said, "Let me in Lester."

The door opened. Lester stood aside as his father walked past him. No word was exchanged.

Mr. Klopper walked around the room, jingling the change in his pocket. He stopped at the bookshelves lining the wall and read a few titles. He turned from them and glanced about the room, at the maps on the wall, the pictures of far-off places cut from magazines and pinned up. He saw a desk, a bed, a radio, a chair, books and pictures. No models, no pennants, no sports. The room of a roaming mind and incapable body. He looked around as if he were a stranger to it.

He walked over to the window, looked out and pulled the window shade up and down a few times. Lester sat on his bed.

Finally, with a jerk of his head indicating the door, Mr. Klopper said, "You heard?" His back was still turned.

Lester murmured, barely audible, "I'm sorry, Pa."

He was putting into those few words more than being sorry for what he had heard, more than understanding about his absent and no-father father. He was trying to say he was sorry for what he was. He was sorry for the disappointment he must be. Tears welled and rolled as he looked dumbly over to the man at the window. Under the fear and behind the resentment had always been this longing to be able, finally, to say just that: I'm sorry, Pa. Sorry I'm this way. Sorry I can't make you love me, sorry I'm alive.

Mr. Klopper wasn't about to talk about it. He dismissed it with a rough gesture and a deep sigh. "That's done and over with. Water under the bridge." He stopped fiddling with the window cord and sat on the bed beside Lester.

"Your mother told me about yesterday," he said. "Any news about that boy Alfred? How is he?"

"No, Pa." Lester shook his head, miserable. "I don't know anything. Except it was my fault. I took him there."

His father grunted. "Fault, schmault. Maybe it was. But I hear you got him out of the train. Out of that train by yourself. Right?"

Lester nodded.

Mr. Klopper slapped his knees and stood up. "In my opinion that was *some* business. In my opinion that's what I call acting like a *mensch!*"

Lester raised his head to look at his father's face, to take in the words his father had said. His father had called him . . . *him* a *mensch.* There was a time he would have sold his soul to hear those words. But now they didn't matter.

"So tell me, are you going to stay in this room the rest of your life? I want my supper."

Lester, who was never able to talk in front of his father, spoke now from the depths. "Pa, nobody helped. People were there. In the train. They saw and nobody helped me." He had to stop and swallow a few times in order to go on. At last he brought it out. "People are rotten," he said. "I don't want to come out of this room. What for?"

His father looked down on him, those telltale eyebrows raised in surprise at what he had heard from his usually silent son. He began pacing the room again, picking his

97

way carefully through the words, finding it difficult to express his meaning. He was unaccustomed to speaking seriously with Lester.

"So people are rotten, you say? What can I tell you, Lester? That's not exactly news to me. Listen. In my business I've seen things, things that would make your hair curl. Lying and cheating and all the rest. Fear, that's it. That's the bottom line. Fear kept those people in their seats. But . . . ." He stopped his pacing to face his son sitting so woefully on the bed. "But I've also seen things that would surprise you. People scrimping dimes to see that their families are taken care of. People you would think are trash, doing . . . wonderful things. And not just for their own sakes. I've been amazed—plenty of times! Sure people can be rotten. But at the same time people can be . . . good. A little of both, son, a little of both." He spread his fingers, tipping his hand back and forth. "Rotten and good. Just like me, Lester. And like your mother . . . and you . . . and maybe everyone else you know. You grow up and learn that."

"Not Alfred, Pa!"

"Well, he's a special case then. What we'll do is have supper before I faint from hunger and your mother makes a swimming pool out of my bed with her crying. Then we'll call over to your friend's house, and we'll find out what's with him."

He walked to the door, opened it and said, "Let's go."

Lester followed his father out of the room.

There wasn't any news of Alfred that night. The Burts were not home. Aunt Ida told them that Alfred's parents were still at the hospital. No, there wasn't any diagnosis yet. Tests were still being made.

Lester was still eating his breakfast the next morning when the telephone rang. It was Myron. He and Claire wanted to come see him. Could they?

"Sure," said Lester.

Myron and Claire were relieved to see him and dying to hear what had happened.

"We tried to see you all day yesterday, hey Les." Myron lowered his voice and glanced at the closed door. "Your Ma sure sounded funny on the phone. She said you weren't feeling so good. You okay now?"

As he said this, he walked across the room to sit on the bed beside Lester. His sneaker caught in the fringes of the rug. To save himself from falling, he made a wild grab at the standing lamp beside the chair. He didn't quite reach it. The brush of his fingers was enough to send the lamp crashing to the floor, and he sprawled face down across the arms of the chair.

A knock on the door. "What's going on in there?" Mrs. Klopper demanded.

"Nothing, Ma. Everything's okay."

Lester and Claire had the giggles while Myron straightened the damage and sat carefully on the chair. "My mother doesn't call me klutz for nothing," he said sheepishly, grinning at the two of them.

The laughter cleared the air and Lester felt much better. Claire bounced on the bed and said, "C'mon, tell. All we know is that you and Alfie were in the train and something happened to him and you got him out of the train. You're a hero, you are. It's all over the building."

99

"Some hero!" said Lester grimly, remembering his utter panic.

He then started at the beginning and just when he got to the part about stealing the oarlocks he stopped and groaned. Only in the telling did he realize the oarlocks were left on the train.

"Oh, Myron! All for nothing!" He was appalled.

"What is? Oh, never mind, just go on."

Lester steadied himself and took them through the rest of the day, stealing the oarlocks, Frankie and the picnic and then the awful time on the train.

When he finished they all sat in silence for a while.

"Wow!" whispered Claire.

"Yeah," said Myron with reverence.

They looked at their friend with new eyes. What they felt most deeply was surprise. Lester had surprised them. They hadn't realized until that moment that they had a different set of expectations for him than they had for themselves. They thought they had him pegged and now he had upset all that.

They took him back over the whole day again, wanting to hear every detail. How could he possibly have dragged Alfie out of that train? Neither of them could get over the fact that just he and Alfie had risked so much to get the oarlocks and had actually walked away with them.

"You're a double hero!" declared Claire. "I'm going to tell all my friends."

"Hey, not on your life! Don't advertise it please. You didn't know I was a thief did you?" grinned Lester. "The Spastic Cat strikes again! Next time I'll try jewels."

"You bet," said Myron, sitting now on the arm of the

chair, bending it with his weight. "I'll help you and probably swallow them by mistake."

"That's okay. We can get them again the next morning," said Lester slyly.

Myron was hiding from the others how greedy he felt for those oarlocks now that he learned they were almost in his grasp. His teeth hurt he wanted them so much. He had a sudden vision of himself running madly through all the trains, pushing people aside, searching for the shopping bag.

He described to Lester a different way to hold the oars in place. "I just drilled a hole on each side of the boat and put a solid piece of wood there sticking up. When I pull on the oars that'll hold them all right. It's not great, but it's okay. I don't need oarlocks."

"What do you suppose is the matter with Alfie?" Claire at last brought up what they had been avoiding.

There was an uneasy silence.

Finally, Myron stood up and said, "Let's go see if Mrs. Burt is home. We've got to find out."

Lester twisted around on the bed. He wanted to look only at a wall. "I don't think I can face her," he said. "She'll blame me. She'll think it was my fault, and it was, it was!"

"Shut up, Les," said Claire firmly. "You got him out of the train and that's that. Maybe he just fainted or something." That idea cheered them all up considerably. "C'mon, get up. Let's go, right now."

"Right, Claire," said Myron.

As the three of them left the room, Lester noticed Myron's appreciative look at Claire.

He's not so blind any more, thought Lester.

Chapter Thirteen

The three walked slowly down the street, headed for the last building on the block. Beyond it stretched the large empty sand lot covered with scrub, a favorite place for smoking forbidden cigarettes or roasting mickeys whenever anyone was lucky enough to smuggle some potatoes out of the house. Acrosss the street, the schoolyard was full of action as always. Lester could see the very spot near the fence where he had met Alfred not so long ago.

Claire tried to curb her natural swiftness for Lester's sake, while Myron slowly ambled beside him like a blond bear. The boys watched Claire run around each spindly tree lining the sidewalk. In her usual outfit of running shorts and T-shirt she was a white arrow of energy. She could see the boys found her detours amusing. Annoyed, she said, "Well, the regionals are coming up, smarties, and if you want to watch me win that race, you better wipe those smiles off."

"You tell 'em, girlie," called an old man sitting on a folding chair, enjoying the sun with his cronies.

"That's a girlie?" said another. The small group around him wheezed and chuckled with him.

"I wasn't laughing at you, Claire." Myron hoped she hadn't heard the comment.

"I was," said Lester, enjoying his growing taste for teasing.

Claire pretended to lunge at him, then sprinted down the block to wait for them in front of Alfred's building.

Instead of going straight upstairs to see Mrs. Burt, Myron first wanted to show Lester something in the paint room. A surprise he said it was. At this, Claire, who had forgotten, bounced up and down and squealed, "Wait'll you see!"

What they had to show him was the boat, finished, painted, ready for launching.

"We worked for two days straight, didn't we, Claire?"

She was no longer with them. She was searching the basement for Mr. Moskowitz.

Myron walked around the boat brushing the sides with his fingertips, loverlike. Lester stood in the doorway amazed at what they had done. It looked so different now that it was rubbed smooth and painted. It looked like a real boat—almost. It sat on the two sawhorses, the bright green of the new paint seeming to light up the gloomy paint room. Boards had been put in for seats, supports for the oars nailed in and even the oars were newly painted and ready.

Lester walked around the boat taking it all in. On the side, in blazing yellow, was printed the name: THE GETAWAY.

"Beautiful!" said Lester. Once again. "Beautiful!"

"Who, me?" asked Claire, returning with the cat in her arms. "Isn't it something?!" She and the boys looked down at the boat like doting parents.

Lester said, "When are you going to do it, My? I mean, when is the launching?"

"I dunno." He was itching to shoulder the boat that very minute and hustle it down to the beach and slip it into the water. He had dreamed about the launching for so long, dreamed about getting it out there, far out in the ocean, for such a long time. He could see himself on the shore looking out to the tiny figure that was also Myron, bobbing up and down in the distance. Claire, Lester and Alfie were with him on the beach, also watching that tiny figure. Then he switched to the self in the boat. The oars were shipped and his arms rested on them as he looked back to shore. He felt the distance and the peace, the lack of connection with anything back there. Only now could he make out the figures on shore watching for him and waiting for him. Now there were connections on shore he didn't want to leave. He felt all muddled.

"I dunno," he repeated and turning to Claire, "when do you think? Tomorrow maybe?"

Again he saw them all on shore waving good-by to him as he rowed *The Getaway* out, slicing the water, putting distance between them. Well, he would take it out for a little while and then return for them one at a time. First Claire, then Lester, then Alfie. Alfie!

"I know," he said, feeling certain. "We'll launch it as soon as Alfie gets home. It's only right that he's there too, whattaya think?"

That seemed like a perfect idea. Surely they could wait a day or so until he got back.

Elated, they went upstairs to ring Mrs. Burt's bell, convinced it would cheer her up to know what was in store for Alfie when he returned.

Mrs. Burt opened the door. Lester could see she had been crying and all the elation drained out of him. She was cordial as she invited them in, but the sight of her swollen eyes made him shiver with guilt and regret. Just lowering himself to a chair in the living room was a chore. He fought to control his breathing, to quiet himself.

"I'm glad to see you are up and around, Lester," Mrs. Burt said. The three friends were sitting on the couch, facing her. Her chair was near the window and the strong daylight showed a face drained of color, even of emotion.

"We spoke to your mother and she told us what you did for Alfie. I want to thank you." She saw that Lester was trying to speak and raised her hand to stop him. As if she knew exactly what he was about to say, she continued, "No, no, it wasn't your fault in any way. He had one of those attacks one time before. We were hoping it was just that once." Her mouth twisted, but otherwise she was entirely composed.

Lester was too caught up to feel anything like relief just then. There was something about her voice and manner that was different. Not just worry or sadness, something else.

Claire was the one to ask directly about Alfred. What was the matter with him? How was he?

Completely matter-of-fact, Mrs. Burt told them that she had gotten a call from the hospital that morning. The test results were in. She was waiting for her husband to come home so they could go to the hospital and talk about it with the doctor. What she knew now was that Alfred had some form of epilepsy.

"Epilepsy? What's that?" What a word. It didn't sound at all like anything they knew like . . . flu . . . tonsillitis, bellyache, cerebral palsy. . . .

She told them she didn't know much about it either. She shook her head, her soft brown eyes turned away from them, searching for something out the window that was far, far away. "The doctor said that something goes wrong with his brain once in a while. He said I should think of it like a short circuit, whatever that means. He said that Alfie has these seizures and will go on having seizures until they find the right drugs to give him. There's nothing to do for it, no operation or anything. Just certain drugs, and it's only a maybe that the drugs will work." She fell silent, still searching the distance.

Myron cleared his throat and said, "Seizures? You mean like . . . fits?" Fits he had heard of.

Claire glared at him, thinking that was an awful word to say to Mrs. Burt. It was a word of fun and ridicule. But it didn't affect Alfie's mother one way or the other.

Again Lester sensed something missing that had been a part of her before.

"Yes, Myron, 'fits,' " she said quietly. "Seizures, epilepsy. Now we know. It wasn't enough my boy is crippled and retarded. He has to have epilepsy, too." Another flat statement.

Aunt Ida bustled in from the kitchen with a tray of lemonade and honey cake. Hearing what her sister just said, she put down the tray on top of the big Zenith radio and, raising her voice, she scolded her. "What a way to talk! Florrie, that boy's going to be fine. I never heard you say that before. He's not retarded. He's a little slow, but not retarded! I'm surprised at you. They'll find something to cure him in that hospital and he's going to be just fine. You'll see. Just fine."

Mrs. Burt turned her eyes to her sister and Lester felt the cold sweep through him. He had never seen such a look before.

"Don't be a fool, Ida," she said. She wasn't angry, she wasn't upset. There was only bitter certainty in what she said next. "Alfie is not fine and will never be fine and that's that. Don't talk to me of fine anymore. His father knew this all along, and now . . . I know it."

Now Lester knew what was different about her, what was missing. It was hope.

"Isn't he coming home, Mrs. Burt?" asked Claire as softly as she could. She didn't know what question would be all right to ask.

"Yes, he'll be coming home, Claire, but we don't know when. He'll stay in the hospital for a while, the doctor says. They have to decide what drugs to use." She passed her hand over her hair, smoothing it, an absent-minded gesture of habit, without vanity.

Lester hadn't spoken a word until then, but he needed to ask, "What is going to happen to Alfie, Mrs. Burt?" He hardly knew what he meant. He wanted to know if he was going to have his friend back again. He wanted to know the impossible. He wanted to know the future.

Mrs. Burt spoke just to him, as if no one else was in the room. "Lester, I don't know. 'What's going to happen to Alfie?' That's all I think of now. All the time. All I can tell you is my boy isn't sick enough to be put away and he's not well enough to be home. That's the only thing I know."

The words hung in the air. No one had anything to say

in the face of such an unimaginable dilemma.

To their relief, Richy came bouncing into the room, radiating health and ready for play. He tackled Myron, throwing himself at his legs to pull him off the chair. "Gotcha!" he laughed. It was as if the sun had come out.

Mrs. Burt was the only one not smiling. "Go play with Sheldon, Richy. We're talking."

"Aw Mom, Myron's here. I don't wanna play with Sheldon. I cheat on him and he don't even know. We play cards and I cheat on him easy, I don't even hide it and he goes on playing. What a dumbbell!" He was gleeful.

His mother stood up, suddenly shaken into anger. "Don't you call him a dumbbell! I don't want to hear you call *anyone* a dumbbell, ever. You hear me? Now go play in your room if you won't play with Sheldon. Not here." Her finger pointed him out of the living room and into the hall.

Richy, still full of good humor, spread his arms out and, making propeller sounds with his lips, flew his airplane around the room. He dipped his wings around each chair and then sped down the hall still buzzing the airfield.

Watching Mrs. Burt through all this, Myron had a whiff of something new to him. Carefully, he said to her, "That's a nice boy you got there, Mrs. Burt."

Mrs. Burt was her collected self again. She glanced at the hallway where her son had disappeared and said politely, "Thank you, Myron. Yes, he's a good boy."

There was something funny in the way she was with the kid, Myron realized. But why? She wasn't a mean lady at all. Could grownups also have feelings they couldn't control or understand? He thought you grew out of that. He thought of his mother, leaning on him, screaming at him because he wasn't what she wanted him to be. He hadn't thought of it from her point at all. And if his father hadn't died . . .?

Claire and Lester were standing up, so Myron got up, too.

Aunt Ida, still brooding over her sister's reproof, collected the glasses and the empty dish of cakes and went off to the kitchen in silence. Mrs. Burt walked them to the door.

Claire said, "So I guess Alfie won't be here for the launching, huh, Mrs. Burt?"

"Oh, is the boat ready? That's wonderful." There was a touch of her old warmth. "I'll tell Alfie. I just don't know when he'll be home, so you better just go ahead with it. But he'll be glad to hear about it." She opened the door.

"Tell him we want him back," said Lester. Mrs. Burt took his hand so tenderly and smiled such a sad smile he thought his heart would break. "I'll do that, Lester."

They exchanged good-bys and the door was closing behind them, when Claire put her hand out to stop it. "Wait a minute, Mrs. Burt." To Myron she said, "What about having the launching tomorrow, hey? It's Saturday so my mom can come and my dad can help carry the boat to the water. Yeah. Why not?" She turned back to Mrs. Burt. "Can you come? Can you? You and Richy and everyone! What do you think, My?"

Myron already saw it all happening. "Okay. Okay now, that's it. Tomorrow. What do you say, Les?"

Lester said yes with his head, his heart, his whole body. He looked beseechingly at Mrs. Burt. She answered that look. "I'd love to come. We'll just have to see. Maybe, if it's in the morning. We go to the hospital in the afternoon. Call us and let us know. I'd love to. Really I would."

"Okay, then, tomorrow morning," said Myron.

Chapter Fourteen

I was up and out the door this morning before the deep freeze in my house made my nose drop off. The few words my Ma and Pa said to one another outside my door the other night did it. They haven't said a word to each other since. I'm the new messenger boy around here. Last night for instance. "Tell your father supper is on the table." Pa is not in Russia, he's sitting right there in his easy chair reading the paper. "Tell your mother I'm not hungry." Sure, Pa, but I guess I'll have to use sign language. She must have turned stone deaf, since she's standing right here beside me.

It's no fun being the middleman, I can tell you. They are using me to get at one another. All of a sudden I'm the prize in the Crackerjacks. Not so long ago I was the invisible man to one and the hair shirt to the other. Now at least I'm a someone *else*, so I guess I like it better.

I thought at first after our talk that things would be really different between my father and me. As usual, my fantasies ran wild and I saw us going arm and arm into the sunset. Or at least having confidential little chats before bedtime, deep silent chess games, outings . . . . I'm such a child, really. Well, old habits are hard to break, I guess. I asked him if he would like to come to the launching today, but he was sorry, he had promised to visit a friend. Huh and humph. But even so, I'm not complaining. I know that things are a *little* different between us. It's a start, anyhow.

I asked Ma if she would like to come to the beach to watch the launching. Now there's a different story. You'd think she was a schoolgirl and I, the football hero, had asked her to the prom. She actually flushed when she said she would very much like to come. Her eagerness made me feel so bad. I hadn't realized how much I had turned away from her. I touched her arm and kissed her cheek and told her where to meet us and all, thinking all the while that I hadn't meant to shut her out all this boat summer. All this Alfred summer. It just worked out that way.

Anyway, I was up and out of the house early this morning. Myron's mother answered the doorbell, still in her bathrobe. It's a good thing Myron is a boy. He looks just like his mother only all that beefiness doesn't look as good on her.

"Come in, Lester," she said. "Myron isn't here, can you imagine? This time of the morning and he's downstairs with that boat of his? He had to do some last minute thing to the boat, he says, before even getting the rolls from the store. We had to do without!"

All the time she's talking, talking, I'm following her not knowing what else to do. She's talking to me over her shoulder, so I can't just leave her and go into the living room and sit. She walked into the kitchen and like the little lamb that I am, I went too.

At the table eating breakfast are the twins. All I know about them is that they giggle a lot and tease the daylights out of Myron. Now I see that they can eat, too. As my mother would say, "God bless them, they can eat." Cold cereal boxes were opened on the table and they were attacking mounds of eggs, onions and lox, all scrambled together. A vision in tutti-frutti. Their appetite made me slightly nauseous. Fortunately, I was about as interesting to them as the single sodden cornflake left in the bowl. They didn't say anything to me, so I didn't have to say anything to them.

"Sit down, Lester," said Mrs. Kagan. "Have a little something."

"No thanks, I had breakfast."

I was about to go downstairs to look for Myron when he burst into the kitchen, loud and rough with excitement, like a charging bull. He was aglow with it, his face redder than usual, his eyes lit up. He lunged at me and I didn't know whether to cry "Watch out!" and throw myself under the table or hold my ground and let him grab me. Like a true soldier, I stood my ground. He gripped my arm. I winced.

"Wait'll you see, Lester! C'mon downstairs, I gotta show you something," he said, pleased out of his skull. Suddenly he noticed his mother and sisters, as if they had just dropped from the ceiling.

"Hey, you're still in your bathrobes!" he cried. "Put some clothes on. We're going to get it to the beach soon. You wanna be late?"

His mother pushed him out of the kitchen saying, "Go, Myron, go. Don't you worry. It's still early. You haven't gotten that boat out of the basement yet. How you're going to do that without tearing the building down, I don't know. We have lots of time."

First she was pushing and then she grabbed at his shirt to hold him back. "No, wait a minute. I said we have lots of time. Plenty of time for you to go to the cleaners for me first. I have a bundle there." She was rummaging around in her pocketbook looking for the ticket.

I waited for the whining, for the explosion. But nothing like that happened.

He touched her arm to stop the searching. Very firmly he said, "Not now, Ma," and he was out the door. On the way down we stopped the elevator at the fourth floor to call for Claire. She was waiting for us and so was her father. I hadn't met him before. He and Claire kept fooling around together as they got ready. Lucky Claire.

We got back in the elevator and when we passed the third floor I thought of Alfie and the Burts. Alfie should be with us today.

As I stepped into the basement I took a deep breath. At first I couldn't see what Myron had done that was so special. The boat looked exactly the same as it had yesterday. Myron just stood aside with his arms crossed and let us find out for ourselves. I circled the boat and saw it. What he had done was to cross out the name and give it a new one. He didn't paint over it, he had actually made a line through it and left it. What you saw was:

THE ~~GETAWAY~~ ALFRED

"See? Now everyone can see that we changed it," said Myron. "It's for him. What do you think?"

He looked first to Claire, as always. She bit her lip and

114

nodded yes. Somebody should look at me like that someday.

As for me, I could have kissed him. "He'll like it, My.
It's a good idea." I could just imagine Alfie's face when
we told him. It would take him a minute to get it. Then
he would throw back his head, clasp his bad hand to his
chest, giving himself over completely to the laughter. He
was a good laugher. I mean he *is* a good laugher.

Well, then we started to figure out how to get the boat
out of the basement.

It wasn't such a big deal after all. Just a small matter
of taking the door off of the paint room, getting the super
to help lift and turn the boat and an hour or so of dirty,
sweaty, anxious work.

"Whatcha got here, Myron, the *Queen Mary?*" the
super growled when he first lifted it. "Betcha that liner
doesn't weigh as much as this tub." He never took the
cigar out of his mouth, and he grumbled every inch of
the way. I don't know how he managed it. Nevertheless
he was helpful and I don't think we could have done it
without him.

I, of course, was essential. Would this country have
been settled without the advance scouts? Would the boat
party know they were coming to a corner unless I told
them?

Finally, finally, it was out and done. It rested in front
of the house while Myron yelled up to the top floor for
his mother and sisters. With a voice like that he could
have summoned President Roosevelt from Washington.
He also shouted for Mrs. Burt. She leaned out of the
window, waved and called down, "Coming!"

Meanwhile, the boat was getting quite a bit of attention. Richy and a bunch of his friends crowded around oohing and aahing. So were lots of other people from the building. Crowds seem to attract crowds, and soon the kids from the schoolyard across the street came over to see what was going on.

When the word went around that the boat was about to be carried to the beach and launched, it was as if everyone had been invited to the same party at the last minute. I heard arrangements being made on all sides. Kids were calling up to their mothers getting permission to go to the beach. Side bets were being made on whether or not "that thing" would float. Mothers were bringing out strollers to push the littler kids. While this hubbub was going on, the Burts and Myron's family came out of the building and we were ready to go.

What a procession! In front was the boat, carried by four pallbearers, one for each end. They carried it on their shoulders as if they were going to bury it instead of launch it. Surging behind were the merry mourners.

Fortunately it was a slow parade, so I was able to keep up. Claire walked along with me, carrying the oars. Myron was everywhere, like a herding sheepdog.

As we went by, the jokers, onlookers lining the sidewalk, called out, "Something dead in there?" or "Get a horse, it would float better." Things like that. The crowd laughed at everything. It felt as if the boat was carried along on a wave of good humor. Claire and I kept giggling at one another. We never thought it would be like this. Whenever we looked ahead to the launching, it was always just the four of us. Not the whole of Brooklyn.

We had two long blocks of this and then, across the

wide avenue, stopping traffic, waiting for the trolley to pass. Then one block over to the free beach.

When we got there, Myron couldn't wait to see whether the ocean was rough or smooth. He dashed ahead, across the sand, and stood looking out over the water. The boat was carried across the beach and ceremoniously placed at the water's edge. Claire handed Myron the oars. The rest of us, the whole crowd, settled down on the sand to watch, as if waiting for the curtain to go up on a play.

Mr. and Mrs. Burt came over to where I was sitting with Ma and Claire.

"Do you mind if we sit with you?" Mrs. Burt asked. Mind? If I knew how to grovel, I would have. She said she noticed the name of the boat and that she thought it was very sweet of us.

"Yes," agreed Mr. Burt. "Thank you. Alfred will like that. He'll be wanting to hear everything about this when we see him this afternoon." Claire told them it was Myron's idea, though I would have loved to keep the credit.

There was no more talk because from then on neither Claire nor I took our eyes from Myron. We could imagine how nervous he was with all these people watching.

The ocean seemed to be waiting, so calm it was. Small waves lapped at the boat, tame as pussycats. It was one of those summer days with the sun so warm and the air so fresh you felt any other kind of day was a terrible mistake.

The crowd grew quiet, knowing the action was about to begin. Myron waved to us, put the oars in the boat and pushed off. He climbed in when it was afloat and then he was off and paddling.

It didn't take long. I guess maybe it was all over in five minutes at the most. He was facing us, rowing furiously for the horizon. And before our eyes, Myron's body began to sink lower and lower, because the boat was sinking lower and lower. He just kept on rowing, rowing, concentrating entirely on just doing that. Soon the water was up to the very edge of the boat, then it poured in, and still he rowed. We could all see the look of utter bewilderment on his face when he realized he was up to his armpits in water, holding two oars and the boat gone.

What a roar from the crowd. Laugh? They were still laughing when Myron emerged from his swim back. He stepped doggedly out of the shallow water and on up the beach without raising his eyes.

It was a terrible moment. Don't think the irony of *The Alfred* sinking escaped me and I'm not big on symbols usually. I stole a quick look at Mrs. Burt. She was looking around, distressed for Myron's sake, trying to hush the people around us who were getting such a kick out of the whole thing.

Everyone now was hooting and catcalling, laughing at him, enjoying the disaster much more than they would have enjoyed the success. Or so it seemed to me. Mostly they were laughing at Myron because he looked so foolish, so woebegone, so terribly embarrassed.

He stood there at the water's edge, dripping wet, as if listening to a sentence, the crowd the jury. I thought to myself that this was going to really do it for Myron. Now he surely will want to get away forever.

I saw him look at Claire. Then, incredibly, he smiled at his audience and raised his arms. He clasped his hands over his head in a victory salute. He shook his hands overhead, turning this way and that. Then he bowed as if acknowledging applause and again lifted his arms.

Suddenly, the whole mood changed. Myron changed it. Somehow it was such a ridiculous thing to do, the crowd loved it. Laughter swept across the crowd once again, and then applause. But now the laughter was completely *for* him instead of at him.

"Attaboy Myron!" shouted Claire.

I couldn't believe it. I looked around at Myron's family and my own ma clapping away. I listened to that big crowd appreciating my friend when just a moment before they were hurting him. I saw Myron's big dopey grin and knew his heart had gone down with his boat. I saw the Burts cheering as if they hadn't a care in the world. And I didn't forget me, either, unable to even do a decent job of yelling for my friend and yet bursting with . . . I don't know what.

Really, sometimes life just knocks me out!